Bill

Certainly not of Kev[...]
quality, but I hope you
enjoy this as you continue your
exploration of the Odd West.

J Bi [signature]

MW01532994

ONE STEP
FROM GLORY

syptnichols@gmail.com

Bill

I enjoyed visiting you about our common interest, Western novels. Thanks for sharing time with me and showing me your collection. I am going to tell Kelton's niece here in Marshall about it when I have a chance.

Last October Paula and I went to Ruidoso, NM and attended the Cowboy Symposium (has a website). If you like cowboy music, chuck wagons, horses, etc., I would recommend it to you. Thousands attend it every year.

Bill

ONE STEP FROM GLORY

By

J. Brian Nichols

This is a work of fiction. All the characters and events portrayed in this book are either products of the author's imagination or are used fictitiously.

ONE STEP FROM GLORY

ISBN 0-9721845-9-7

Published By
Painted Word Studios
Crosby, Texas
U.S.A.

Foreword

My dad was a cowboy at heart. Although he lived most of his adult years in the city, he thrilled me as I was growing up telling about his exploits with a rope and his favorite horse, Roxie. Much contained in this book describes my recollection of stories he told others and me in my family prior to his untimely death in 1995.

Dad always said he wanted to write a western novel. Since that never happened, I took it upon myself to write it for him. This is my first stab at book writing. Oh, I shudder to think what he would say if he read this book because he was such a perfectionist. He'd probably say it was too short, or too shallow, or didn't contain enough descriptive literature, or something else. After all, that's what he'd do to even the best of writers, like his favorite, Zane Grey. He'd probably want me to rewrite it over and over again. From that standpoint, I'm glad he won't be scrutinizing it. On the other hand, I wish I could now look into his eyes as he read my book and catch a sense of his satisfaction that I was actually following in his footsteps in my love for western lore.

I'm not sure how "real" western novelists make plans for writing their books. I just developed a general outline of what I envisioned, and let pure inspiration guide me from there. It evolved into part novel, and part description of some of what I know about the Nichols family. Parts are authentic, while others are simply figments of my imagination. For instance, the characters discussed in Chapter One, and sporadically thereafter, are meant to be the actual Nichols family, with dad, as a boy, being the narrator. Conversely, the central storyteller, Grandpa, never made it to Texas, as far as I know.

And throughout the book you'll see the same pattern. There are instances of stories I've heard, and others that merely came to my mind at the time.

Another aspect of this book involves its inclusion of details that are tributes to Dad himself. The average reader will pass these situations by, but family members will notice that they were intended to bring back memories, some fond, and some not so fond, of Dad and his antics.

Finally, the book developed into one where the central character, Jeremy "Buck" Ward, displayed an evolving Christian morality, something not often depicted in classic western novels. This occurred at first at my wife's insistence. Then, as I was coerced to continue this theme, I grew to realize that I wanted Buck to display these characteristics as a testimony to others about my family's faith in Jesus Christ.

Acknowledgements

To Gary, Pat and Jill,
the surviving members of the immediate family of
Travis Samuel and Ruby Nichols

And thanks to my loving wife, Paula, for her support and
assistance, and to Richard Fluker, for his technical
expertise.

Introduction

Soon after Dr. Brian Nichols had been named superintendent-elect of Marshall Public Schools, we were at a track meet watching his older daughter run. As our conversation ranged through areas of common interests, he made an intriguing statement. "I don't feel like I've been on vacation unless I've been to the Rockies." I remember immediately thinking to myself, "Here's a man I can enjoy working for."

The "Dr." soon became a title relevant only in official references that I made as the school district's public information officer. In private conversations and away from work, he was "Brian." That initial mention of the Rockies and a love of the West in general led to a common ground we would traverse in many discussions and several times in person. We enjoyed white-water rafting in Colorado, an overnight stay at the bottom of the Grand Canyon, a hike in Big Bend. The first of two marathons he talked me into running was even in Abilene!

Early on Brian regaled me with tales of his father who, as a "cowboy at heart," would pack up the family and head out West. As Brian narrated I would shuffle through the photos of my mind in an effort to locate images of the same or similar places. When he spoke of Monument Valley, Utah, I immediately saw a young Navajo running toward me at the entrance in 1978, eager to sell me some beads. The Mogollon Rim in Arizona? Been there. Hairpin curves near Ouray, Colorado. Ditto. From western state to western state they went, and years later I would wander many of the same roads.

When Brian told me he was writing a Western novel, I had to smile upon learning that the central character was a young Texas cowboy whose dream was to trek from Corsicana (my hometown) to the Rocky Mountains. Buck Ward was drawn in the 1800s by descriptions of their beauty and the promise that they held.

For a different reason and years later, Brian made his first trip and has felt the magnetism of those rocks ever since.

As I read the novel, I envisioned Buck's meanderings from Central Texas out through the Panhandle. His vista of the way out West, of course, was on horseback, while Brian's familiarization with the route came from inside a horseless carriage. But as I read on, I began to sense that a little bit of Brian Nichols was riding in that saddle with Buck. Is it any wonder? A dreamer for a father, a childhood of stories about cowboys, a well-worn collection of Zane Grey novels, abundant retracing of trails imprinted by boots and hooves many years ago. It all adds up. The result is a novel with places that seem real and characters the reader can feel at home with. Did Buck make it to the mountains? Whether or not he did doesn't seem as important as the fact that he had a dream.

I've heard that as we grow older—with careers winding down and children gaining their independence—waning obligations to others allows us to more freely pursue the path of our own dreams, to become our real self. A few years ago Brian built, largely with his own hands, a log home. Inside and all around it are conversation pieces related to the West, to cowboys and the old-fashioned way of life. Now add to it two horses and daily rides around the Nichols "ranch." The trail beckons.

Brian may be Dr. Nichols. But I'm quite sure that beneath all that education and the title is the spirit of someone who'd be proud of another moniker—"Cowboy."

Richard Fluker

Chapter One

The roaring fire in the old rock fireplace cracked loudly as the mesquite embers warmed my backside, though the rest of me was still frigid. Feeding the animals on our forty-acre farm was my job now that I had reached my tenth birthday, and the reality of how hard this task was, especially during the cold winter months, caused me to miss the uncomplicated days of my childhood.

Nevertheless, it was evening now; Mama was cooking a pot of beans on the wood stove, Poppa was finishing up his blacksmithing chores in the makeshift shop he'd built, and Grandpa was sitting in his favorite chair, as always, there in front of the fire.

"Please Grandpa. Tell me another story about when you grew up. P-L-E-A-S-E."

"Aw, boy," Grandpa uttered with his forehead wrinkling profusely, "don't you ever get tired of listening to me spout off? After all, these are the good ol' days, not those days when wild men roamed these parts, more interested in trouble than anything else."

"But Grandpa, just one more. P-L-E-A-S-E. I won't ask you again, I promise."

My grandpa was the best storyteller in them parts. He was the only educated one in our family, and it showed. He knew words that most folks had never heard, and I was constantly havin' to ask him what somethin' meant. "Shucks," I once bragged, "my grandpa knows more words than Mr. Webster himself."

As Grandpa pondered his next response my mind wandered in reckless abandon. I quickly thought back a couple of years to my family's departure from Mississippi. I never really understood why Poppa insisted on coming to Texas. We had a comfortable life there and Mama was really happy. Her well-to-do family had overcome its resistance to her marriage into a lower-class one, and we had actually grown to become well respected there.

I can still hear Grandma Mitchell saying, "You owe her the finer things in life. How do you expect her to make it in that God-forsaken country?"

Poppa said nothing to this, grimaced as he walked away, and told us three boys to, "Start packin' up the belongin's." Later he went to town and bought Mama a new brown grip, one that anyone of high society there in Sherman would be proud of. He gave it to Mama with a big bow tied to it and told her to be sure to pack her "frilly" things in it.

Mama would have gone anywhere with Poppa. They had a storybook romance, and the pleas of her family had no effect on her. She would go to Texas, and she would do her best to make life for us boys and my lone sister a good one.

Grandpa broke my train of thought, saying, "Did I ever tell you about young Buck Ward, a buddy of mine from the war days?"

"No Grandpa," I said excitedly. "Was he a real gun-totin' cowboy?"

"He sure was, son. Just as much as Hardin or Garrett, or any of those others."

My face lit up with anticipation of another one of Grandpa's stories. He'd told me several to that point, and each and every one of them kept me excited to the end. In fact, our trip from Mississippi in the old Model T Ford was made somewhat more bearable because of these stories. Grandpa would sense my childish restlessness and would start telling a tale. At first, he did so just to quiet me. Then, as we bumped along and tried to fight the terrible heat and humidity, he'd begin enjoying the yarn himself. Before long, the whole family would be caught up with anticipation. It sure made the longest car trip of my life bearable.

"But before I commence about Buck you need to finish your chores," Grandpa said with a stern look. I knew when he gave me that look he'd bested me in some way. "Now

2

get back out to that barn and put that saddle and tack up the right way. It's got to last us a long time, and I'll bet you just threw it over in the corner."

"But Grandpa, I don't . . ." I never got anything else out.

"Do you want to hear the story?" he said with a determined look on his face.

"Yes sir," I said as I grabbed my coat and ran out the door.

There was somethin' about grownups that I could never figger out in them days. How did they know when you were up to somethin'? How did they know when you were lyin'? How did Grandpa know that I'd cut corners in doin' my chores that night?

The air was cold and icy as I stepped onto the rickety old porch. I hopped over the broken board about a foot from the first step down and landed on the ground, a good three feet down. I would do the job right, but I was certainly not going to waste any time. For one thing, it was too cold to spend a lot of time doin' what I should have done in the first place. Besides that, the longer I took, the longer I'd have to wait to hear Grandpa's story.

I quickly ran the fifty yards or so to the newly built barn where the animals were kept. It took most of my strength to open the big double doors wide enough to squeeze in. This barn was Poppa's prized possession. He, the other boys, Grandpa and I had erected it right before winter set in. It was built from the finest timber around them parts, and was a good deal nicer than the house we lived in. Mama once remarked that, "For what we spent on this barn we could have remodeled the house." Poppa replied, "But then the animals would have to sleep in here with us." Everyone laughed except Ma.

It was no secret in them days that the farm animals got treated almost as good as us kids, and sometimes better. Bessy was the milk cow, and she had a stall all to herself, made cozy by a deep layer of fresh hay that I'd just put there. She flicked her tail and turned her head toward me as

I entered her abode. She looked at me as if to say, "What ya doing back so soon?"

Roxie, my dapple-gray mare, neighed gently as I tapped her on her nose on my way to the tack area. I'd already spent many hours atop her back, so much so that one neighbor told Poppa that I reminded him of a young Indian boy, almost appearing physically attached to her as I rode by almost every day on my way to school. "Sam," he said one day, "That boy's never going to take to schoolin'. He's a natural-born cowboy, and you'd be better off lettin' him go in that direction."

Mr. Allison was right. Schoolin' didn't set well with me at all. All the time we were supposed to be cipherin' or writin' or whatever the school marm wanted, I was thinkin' about the old west, and how I wished I'd been born during them times. One day, I awoke from a daydream with Miss Molly Murdock standin' over me with a switch, askin' the same question over and over. "Travis, do you know what page we're on? Travis, do you know what page we're on? Travis, do you know what page we're on?" She must have said it several times before I heard because I can still feel the stingin' on my hand as she swatted me three or four times rather hard.

"Yes, ma'am, I know what page we're on!" I replied with a bit of anger in my voice. After all, this didn't make me look too good in Ginny's eyes. Miss Murdock knew embarrassment would work me back in the right direction.

Ginny Wilcox was the prettiest girl in the county. Although she'd never even hinted that she liked me, I had carried on a secret love affair with her for months now. I once even got up enough nerve to talk to her, but she acted entirely uninterested. I guess that's why I had more conversations with my mare, Roxie, than with any other human. I never once got embarrassed by her.

The saddle lay on its side, right where I'd left it, its shiny silver attachments glistening in the faint light of the moon that penetrated the expanse exposed by the open door. I quickly grabbed it up, flung it over the resting post, and reached for the bridle to hang in its place. Finally, I gathered up the sweaty blanket, only minutes from having protected Roxie's back, and placed it upside down over the rail to air out. All this took less than a minute or two, yet I'd earlier tried to avoid doing it to get back to the warm house.

When I was sure that the job had been done properly, I said goodnight to the animals, shoved the two doors together, secured the latch, and ran back to the house as fast as I could.

Mama didn't appreciate the explosion that erupted as I reentered the house. I hit the door on the run and it broke open with a loud bang! "Son, what are you trying to do, destroy what little barrier we've got 'tween us and the elements?"

"I'm sorry Ma, I'm just wantin' to get started on Grandpa's story."

"Well git on over here to the supper table, and he can start on it for all of us," she replied rather shortly, while giving me a slight grin as if to indicate she couldn't wait either.

Mama was a good cook as most women were in them days. Heck, they had to be because most of their responsibilities was cookin', cleanin', mendin' or the like.

That night the table was set with the everyday dishes, not the good ones Mama used for special occasions. The aroma of red beans seasoned with hog jowl caused my mouth to water. And by the time Mama banged the iron skillet on the table to make the cornbread fall loose, I was sittin' quietly in my spot.

Poppa, although not an overly religious man, always insisted on sayin' grace at the table. It was usually somethin' like this. "Lord, we thank you for all of life's blessings. We specially thank you now for these vittles placed before us. Cause us to remember that it's only through hard work that all of our needs will be met. Amen."

I always looked forward to the Amen part because it meant it was time to eat! It was much later in my life that I really took to what the Bible taught. And by then I'd made many mistakes that I wished I could take back. Too bad it's not drawn up that way in the Almighty's plan.

Mama dipped me a bowl of beans first, and then all the others were given their portions. She favored me in this way, and I think some of the other boys resented it. I didn't care though, and I just started eatin' with an eye on Grandpa and the beginnin' of the story.

The long oak plank table didn't suit Ma's elegant taste, but it served the family well. All of us could easily sit around it, with plenty of room still left for the occasional friend, relative, or stranger who happened by at eatin' time.

Poppa occupied the head seat, with Grandpa immediately to his left and Mama to his right. Sister Mary Sue, only five at the time, sat next to Mama so that she could tend to her needs herself. Mama treasured that girl and dreamed of only the best for her. I guess you could say Mama sacrificed her claim on luxury by dreaming of it for her. Next to Mary Sue was Frank, stout as a mule and about as ornery. It was said that no one west of the Mississippi could whip Frank, and he sat out to try to prove it at every available opportunity.

On the other side of the table I always sat beside Grandpa, with Herman, my oldest brother, next to me. Herman could handle a hammer and saw as good as anyone around. Poppa once said that Jesus himself couldn't have built a finer building than Herman, but I always figgered he was jokin'.

Everyone dug into that meal like it might have been their last. You could hear chompin' and smackin' galore, so much so that Mama exclaimed, "Can't you boys act like you been brought up right? Try acting like I've taught you somethin'." But this had only a momentary effect, because in no time at all it sounded just like it had before.

My ears perked up when Grandpa swallowed hard and spoke those words I'd been waitin' for. "I guess I'm filled enough to start my story. Are all of you a'rarin' to listen?"

The clock on the hand-hewn bois d'arc mantle chimed at about that time, yet no one in the room could hear it because of the resounding "YES" that was uttered by everyone at the table. Even Grandpa himself looked like he was lookin' as forward to this as he would have been on his first day of courtin'. In fact, the twinkle in his eye as he began caused me to momentarily forget that he was approachin' the latter days of his life on this earth.

⌘

Chapter Two

The sun was faintly rising in the eastern sky as Jeremy "Buck" Ward mounted the only living thing he trusted, a dark chestnut gelding he called Blaze, and rode off toward the New Mexico high country. It was almost as if an audible voice was calling to Buck to go in that direction. He'd heard it before, but only now was he heeding it. And now, only because of the circumstances he found himself in.

Buck was orphaned at an early age, and found himself passed around from family to family during all of his childhood years. He never knew his mother or father, but was told that they died of the whooping cough when he was less than a year old.

Buck longed to fit in with others, yet every time he seemed to get close to someone, something bad would happen. Once his only friend had taken a fall from his horse and his neck was broken. On another occasion the best foster parent he'd had died suddenly from smallpox. Still another acquaintance befriended him only to betray him in the end by leaving the country with everything of value that he owned. And finally, the one time during his twenty-odd years that he came close to a girl, she ran off with another man while telling him all the while that she loved him.

This last incident had a profound effect on young Buck. He vowed to never get close to another human being. He tried to convince himself that this would be best, yet deep in his heart he yearned for some kind of companionship.

A slight mist began shortly after he crossed Chambers Creek for the first time. This great tributary was more like a river than a creek. Everyone in that part of the country depended upon it for a source of water. It wound about from north to south, then east to west so much that Buck found himself crossing it a half dozen times before he headed northwest for Ft. Worth. He was hoping to make it by the end of the day, but it would be hard traveling to do so.

It was a pleasure to ride Blaze. Part quarter horse and part Arabian, the great chestnut covered ground almost effortlessly. He stood over sixteen hands tall and weighed almost 1200 pounds. His flaxen mane and tail caused him to stand out among other mounts, and more than once Buck had turned down significant offers to sell him.

What would he do without Blaze? He depended on him for transportation. He relied on him to help anticipate trouble. He helped him earn money by winning countless small-time races at county fairs and the like. And finally, Blaze was his best friend. In fact, Buck talked to him as if he were human.

"Blaze," Buck uttered as they loped through a grove of cottonwoods. "I'll bet you could get me to Ft. Worth by sundown if you had a mind to. But, no use, I got nothin' but time, and if I push you too hard I'll really be in a fix."

Buck had always wanted to leave his native Texas for the high country. He'd never been more than fifty miles west of Corsicana, and the only reason he'd ever been out of the state was to serve a stint in the War Between the States. Having survived that ordeal, Buck came back to the area where he was raised and tried to make a life of it.

As rider and horse approached the small hamlet of Boyce, Buck thought about food for the first time since leaving Corsicana. He'd packed a number of biscuits, forty to fifty corn dodgers, plenty of jerky, a little salt pork and enough coffee to last him a while. His pack was quite bulky on the back of his saddle, yet he fully realized that there were many supplies that he would need during the long journey that he simply couldn't carry. For that reason, he planned to hit a town occasionally until he got into Indian country. At that point he knew that it would be he, Blaze and the good Lord who would get him by.

The livery was the first building that caught Buck's eye. He knew he needed to keep Blaze in good shape, so he stopped him right in front of the stable and addressed what appeared to be a stable boy.

"How much for a quart of oats?" questioned Buck.

"I'll be glad to feed, water and brush down your horse for two bits," the boy replied.

"Not likely," Buck said. "He was fed this mornin' and won't be a'needin' anything more 'til sundown. Now how much for the oats?"

Buck was suspicious of this boy just as he was about everyone else he ever encountered. His first thought was that the boy was trying to take him for a fool. After all, he'd never paid to have something like that done in his life. He always did his own work, and he sure didn't trust a stranger to take care of Blaze.

"Three cents," the boy hollered as Buck turned to walk away.

Buck never responded. He'd already decided that he'd wait until he got to Ft. Worth to buy the oats. Maybe he'd get it cheaper there.

There were only four or five buildings in the whole town, and Buck started walking, leading Blaze down the middle of the only street. Wagon ruts were deeply entrenched in the solid black soil that comprised the street. Buck thought that black mud might be one reason why he wanted to get out of this part of the country. He hated trying to walk in it because it would cake up on his boots in a bigger and bigger ball until it was almost impossible to walk. More than once he'd cussed the ground, struggled to get his boots off, and had to walk out of places in his bare feet just to get where he was going.

A dilapidated shack with a cafe sign dangling from only one nail caught his eye as he approached the end of the street. The proprietor was evidently named Danky. It looked like this would be the only place to get a meal here, for all you could see to the northwest where the road headed from there was miles and miles of more blackland. He decided to try it out, despite the unsavory appearance.

The smell of food caught Buck's attention before he ever reached the door. He had to push hard on the door to get it unstuck, thus making enough noise to get everyone's attention in the place.

It appeared that there must be eight or ten tables in the small room he entered; yet it would have only held four or five comfortably. About half of the straw-backed chairs were filled, and a strong aroma of tobacco smoke, liquor and home cookin' confronted him. Buck didn't like this, for he despised those under the influence of strong drink, and eatin' and smokin' just didn't seem to fit together.

Everyone's eyes stared at him as he located the only vacant table. His 6'4" frame had to be squeezed considerably to fit in the chair between the wall and the tabletop.

As he looked up it seemed to him that everyone had stopped what they were doing to gaze at him. There was an old man, probably in his sixties, puffing on a pipe and sittin' with two others about his same age. Coffee cups were scattered about on the table, indicating that they'd been there for a while. At another table, far on the other side of the room sat a younger man, hair as black as pitch and with a scraggly beard, next to a young woman who looked to be no older than Buck. Others in the room quickly turned away from Buck as he began to return their stares.

"What'll you have, mister," came the remark from a homely looking lady with an apron covering her faded and worn out gingham dress. She must have been the proprietor, cook and chief dishwasher all in one. "Special today is beef stew and apple pie."

The thought of apple pie appealed to Buck, even in this less than desirable establishment. Something in his distant memory brought back the sweet smell of apple pie baking and cooling on a windowsill. "I'll have that," Buck replied shortly.

Buck knew that within a short time the luxury of having a store-bought meal would be gone. He also knew that the wages he'd saved and had hidden in a money belt under his buckskin shirt wouldn't last long if he indulged too much. Nevertheless, he felt he should take advantage of this opportunity early in his journey so that he'd be in the best of condition for the challenges that lay ahead.

The lady walked away and headed through swinging doors that obviously led to the kitchen. Because the doors were located close to the table where the man and girl were seated, Buck caught himself giving them more attention than the others.

"Shut up and leave me alone," the man said as he took another drink of whiskey. "That's all you women are good for."

"But please, Will, don't drink any more," the young woman replied.

"I told you to leave me alone." With that the man slapped the girl soundly on the side of the face, a blow that left the girl with a reddened mark.

Buck had seen the effects of strong liquor on men since he was a child. One of his foster parents, a good man when he was sober, resorted to physical violence when he was drunk. More than once Buck had felt the sting of a slap like this one, and he didn't like it one bit. Buck thought that surely someone would come to the defense of the young lady, but the others in the establishment seemed to not notice. It was almost as if they didn't want to get involved.

Buck had a long history of getting involved in these kinds of situations. With the type of raising he'd had, he learned to fight at an early age. As he grew older he developed physically to where he could handle almost anyone who came along. In fact, back home in Corsicana, he was known as Bruisin' Buck, a nickname picked up because of his prowess as a fighter.

Buck had grown to dislike violence, though, after his reputation as a gunman was established. He'd always been good with guns, at first just for the skill of hunting. Buck was known to have been able to strike a match at thirty paces with a 22-caliber rifle. But one day he found himself in a situation where protection was necessary and the young man who challenged him, in a drunken stupor, lay dead on the side of the road. From that day forward Buck was a branded man, and prowess with a gun became a necessity. It was partly for this reason that he had left Corsicana without even telling anyone goodbye. He wanted to escape that kind of life, and his trek to New Mexico was to be the avenue of escape.

When Buck heard the sound of a second slap he knew he could avoid the situation no longer. He slowly rose and calmly walked over to the table where the two were seated. The man was oblivious to Buck's approach, and the girl was sobbing with her head buried on the table.

"Mister," Buck said rather coldly. "I'd appreciate it if you'd stop hittin' this lady. It's beginnin' to ruin my appetite."

Buck always seemed to approach these kinds of troubles with a calm assurance. It probably came about due to his involvement in so many scrapes before. Nevertheless, his cool demeanor seemed to rile those who were the objects of his intent. This proved to be no exception.

The drunken man raised his head from his drink to respond. "I ain't too interested in whether your appetite is bothered or not. Mind your own business."

"Anytime a drunk hits a lady, it's my business," Buck replied with more seriousness.

Buck knew that the coming scuffle would be a short one. Not only did he have confidence in his own abilities, but also the man was quite drunk. His faculties would be impaired, and Buck had already noticed that he was unarmed.

As the black-haired man rose to confront Buck, he almost lost his balance. The girl exclaimed, "Please, mister, let us alone. He really didn't harm me any, and besides, he didn't even realize what he was doin'."

Buck had heard this kind of statement before from those who had been abused. He just couldn't understand why someone would put up with this kind of treatment, and then defend the one doing it.

"I'll leave him alone as soon as you get out of here so I'll know you're safe," came Buck's response.

"OK, OK," she said. "I'll leave." At that, she rushed out the door crying.

Buck hadn't noticed that another man of considerable stature had stood and now was coming toward the table where he and the drunk stood. This somewhat startled Buck, so he quickly turned where he could eye both of them. The man had both hands in a straightforward position and forcefully offered, "Hold it a minute mister. You're about to get mixed up in somethin' you'll regret."

"Well it's clear nobody else was going to take a hand, so it might as well be me," Buck said in response.

About that time the black-haired man took a wild swing at Buck. Buck stepped back quickly, causing the man to fall face first on the floor. This angered him more. He rose again only to meet Buck's powerful fist. The blow knocked him cold. The fight was over.

Those present in the cafe had a look of terror on their faces. The place began to clear out immediately, until only Buck and the man who'd tried to stop the fight remained, standing over the victim.

"Mister, my advice to you is to get out of town fast," the man said. "You just picked a fight with M. B. Bradberry's oldest boy."

"Who's M. B. Bradberry?" Buck asked.

"He owns this town and just about everybody in it. That girl was the boy's wife. You've really stuck your nose in business that weren't yours," he voiced.

"I appreciate your advice," Buck replied. "But it seems to me someone needed to take a stand, and I reckon I'm glad I did. I will take your advice, though. As soon as I eat my meal I'll be gone."

"I hope it's not too late," he stated as he left with the door still standing open.

Buck sensed that he'd stumbled into a real problem. He didn't want trouble here or anywhere else, but it seemed to follow him everywhere he went.

The lady who ran the place appeared and handed Buck a sack. "I took the liberty of packing you a lunch to go. Didn't figger you'd have time to sit and eat."

"Reckon you're probably right ma'am, and thanks. Sorry to have run off all your customers," he said as he reached in his pocket for change to pay her.

"You owe me nothin'," she responded. "I'd have paid you to see that Danny Bradberry whupped. Just watch your backside as you leave town. You won't be safe till you leave the county."

Buck strode outside, took a quick look around, threw the flour sack of food over the McClellan's saddle horn and mounted Blaze. He prompted him with a gentle nudge to the flanks and they were off toward Ft. Worth.

⌘

Chapter Three

Buck didn't particularly like leaving the impression that he was scared off from a place, but he figured leaving would be best. He'd been in town only a short while, disagreed with a boy at the stable, got riled up over a girl's misfortune, had a fight with a drunk, and left without eating to boot. These results left him more determined than ever to spend a life of solitude, traveling alone, and avoiding relationships whenever possible. The far lands of New Mexico continued to call him, and he was going to get there, or die trying.

Buck dreamed of the high country as he passed through the monotonous flatlands leading to Ft. Worth. The territory was mostly blackland farming country, with occasional trees, usually located close to draws or small creeks. Since he thought he might be pursued, he decided to travel off the main road that went northwest from Boyce. He didn't venture far from it though, and he estimated that he lost little time by doing so. Still, it was obvious to him soon that he'd never make Ft. Worth by dark, so he slowed his pace and spoke softly to Blaze.

"Blaze old boy, I now know more'n ever that it's gonna be you and me. Who needs others anyhow? I'm strong, got a good head on my shoulders, at least when I'm not riled, and got nothin' but time on my hands. Other than needing a little dough here an' there, we'll be just fine goin' it alone."

Buck voiced these words with less than a confident tone, for he knew deep down inside that his heart ached for something. Maybe it was for a family that cared for him. It could have been for a close buddy to ride with and tell tall tales to. Or, it could have been the love of a kind, considerate woman, one unlike the girl who left him in the cold a couple of weeks back. Whatever it was, Buck was not to discover it for quite some time.

Several more miles passed before Buck decided to watch for a good spot to camp for the night. Nothing thrilled him like sleeping out under the open stars, with nothing between him and the good Lord but the air itself. He could see a grove of trees in the distance and surmised that there was probably decent grass and water there. Blaze would need both, especially since he'd refused the oats in Boyce.

The sunset in the western sky was only partly visible to him as he gazed through the cottonwoods from a spot he picked. "This looks like it, Blaze," he mumbled as he dismounted in a hurry.

Buck did everything in a hurry. He couldn't stand waiting around much. Maybe that was one reason he was so quick to step in when trouble called. Past experience had taught him that patience was not one of his virtues, and he'd had pretty good results with speed, quickness, and a will to make a difference. He guessed he'd continue in that mode.

Buck began the routine camp tasks before he unsaddled Blaze. He didn't know for sure, but he always figured that it was better to let a mount cool off with the saddle on. So he was able to lay out his pallet, rustle some dry firewood, and get some coffee brewing before tending to Blaze's needs.

As Buck loosened on the cinch and let it drop, it caught briefly on the six-gun protruding from his belt. Buck never took to wearing his gun in a holster on his side. He found that a heavy Colt dangling from a leather belt on his side seemed to slow all his actions down, something that he didn't want. On the contrary, by carrying it tucked into his ordinary belt, it was always ready and waiting for him at a moment's notice. And more than once he'd bested gunslingers that carried them the regular way.

With the saddle and blanket removed from Blaze it was clear to see what a magnificent animal he was. The contrast between his flaxen mane and deep chestnut color seemed to bring out all his best features. The broad expanse between his front legs, his thick, muscled neck, and his enormous hindquarters all revealed his powerfulness. Combined with his overall superior height, it was obvious why Buck revered him so much. Blaze was different than many horses in another way too. He never had to be tied or shackled. Buck simply fed him a handful of corndodgers and let him loose. In the morning he would always be within whistlin' distance.

Buck squatted near the fire as he drank coffee and ate some jerky and a corndodger. It was full dark by now, and the night was going to be cool, particularly so for April in that part of Texas. Perhaps that was another reason why Buck wanted to move on. The durned weather was so unpredictable to him. One day it would be hot as blazes. The next day a blue norther might come in. It prompted Buck once to say that, "Texas weather is like a woman. No one can figger out what she'll do next."

With camp chores completed Buck lay down, gazed at the stars for a few minutes in amazement, and fell off to sleep. He never had trouble sleeping, and could cast almost any thought away at bedtime. He always had the belief that he could worry about those things tomorrow, but for now sleep was what mattered. Tonight was no exception.

Buck slept longer than normal and awoke to the wet nudge of Blaze licking his face. Blaze seemed to always be ready to go on to another place, a little farther than the last time, and this suited Buck well. He rose quickly, remarking to Blaze that, "It's a good thing you woke me up. I might have slept so long that we couldn't make Ft. Worth today." At that he stirred the embers a little, got the coffee pot bubbling again, and set about preparing to leave.

Within thirty minutes of Blaze's coaxing Buck was headed north. He set his sights toward Ft. Worth and determined that he'd only stop a few times during the day to give Blaze a breather. He wanted to get there early in the day.

Buck wondered why he was going out of his way to go through Ft. Worth. Normally he avoided towns if at all possible. After all, it was in these places that trouble seemed to present itself. But why had he almost unconsciously planned to go there?

He tried to dispel the thought that perhaps he wanted to go there to confront, for one last time, the object of his most recent heartbreak, Kelly Stanfield. She was the one who jilted him and ran off with Ned Cole late one night. Buck didn't know about it until he called on her, and her sister, Georgia, gave him the news. He still remembered the feeling that came across him when Georgia said, "I'm sorry Buck, but Kelly left last night with Ned. She told me to tell you good-bye."

Did Kelly honestly believe that a message delivered by her sister would be enough to break the best relationship he'd had over his entire lifetime? How could she have done this anyway? She seemed to really like Buck, and he'd thought that more than a casual relationship was developing.

For more than two hours Buck kept Blaze at a slow lope pace, covering ground smoothly and efficiently. The terrain ahead began to change, with more rolling hills in sight and the emergence of more trees. When he stopped shortly for a rest and water break at a small pool of water, Buck noticed two riders from the south approaching him in a hurry.

The altercation in Boyce seemed a distant memory to Buck now, although it occurred only yesterday. Surely these men weren't after him for that. Maybe they were just heading to Ft. Worth like he was, and they were anxious to get there. He'd know in a minute or two because now he could hear their muffled voices as they approached. Anyway, he'd stand a better chance if he stayed his ground and met them on his own terms.

One of the men was riding a mustang-like pony, his scraggly mane and tail totally unkempt. The other was astride a sorrel, and Buck could see a badge shining in the bright sunlight. It was at this point that Buck sensed trouble.

"Howdy gents," Buck offered as they pulled to a stop about ten paces from him. "Get down and rest a spell."

The men were acting very deliberately as they dismounted. The one with the badge spoke first. "I'm Sheriff Robarbs from Ellis County. I hear tell you attacked a man in Boyce yesterday around noon. Left him in a terrible state, so they say."

"Well that's about the tallest tale I ever heard," Buck responded with the coolness he'd shown before. "I did take a poke at a drunk who was beatin' his wife, and some folks said they was glad I did, kinda like he deserved it."

"Well that drunk, as you called him, filed a complaint in my office, and it's my sworn duty to take you back 'til this here problem gets all cleared up."

Buck surveyed the situation that he found himself in. He could go back and face the law in Boyce for doing something that should have been done a long time ago. Or, he could challenge the sheriff and his deputy right here and now.

Either way Buck figured to lose lots of time on his trek to the New Mexico territory. Based on what he'd heard in Boyce, he'd probably get jail time from a crooked jury bought by Bradberry if he returned. And if he took on the two lawmen now and came out on top, he could be hounded in pursuit by every bounty hunter between here and the New Mexico border.

Buck made his decision pronto, and relayed it to the sheriff by saying, "Sheriff, you look like a good man, but I just plain don't trust you two to see that I get a square deal. My head tells me that a good lawman would not travel this far on a case like this if'n he hadn't been put up to it by someone higher up. I'll bet that someone is M. L. Bradberry."

"Bradberry has nothin' to do with this," the sheriff argued with obvious anger. "Now I don't intend to stand here and argue with you. Put your hands up."

The sheriff's mistake was that he and the deputy had failed to notice Buck's pistol tucked into his pants underneath his coat. The coat's separation allowed Buck to easily reach and draw his firearm before the other two could react for theirs.

"Now gentlemen," Buck voiced. "I'd appreciate it if you'd kindly drop them pistols to the ground."

The men responded as they were ordered to. The sheriff cussed in disgust, and then said, "Stranger, I'll git you for this. You better think again before you take on an official of the state of Texas."

"Meanin' no disrespect sheriff, but I seen enough of you to know that you represent Bradberry more'n you represent my home state," replied Buck. "Now git over to that oak tree, the both of you, pronto."

Buck walked cautiously to where the men were standing by the tree. He took the handcuffs hanging from the deputy's belt and cuffed the men together after he ordered them to reach around the tree and to grasp hands. He then took a rope from the sheriff's saddle, tied the two other hands together, and threw the end over a branch somewhat above their heads. By drawing the rope tight, he now had the men stretched high enough that they'd have difficulty making much movement.

Buck took a look at what he'd done and couldn't help but laugh a little to himself. "You fellers shore look funny, all tied up together. Hope it's not too long before someone comes along to give you a hand," he said as he mounted Blaze and began to ride off.

At that the sheriff let out with a loud string of obscenities, to which Buck paid no mind.

Buck knew that the two men could wrestle free from their predicament within a few hours. However, since he took the keys to the cuffs, they'd be hard pressed to pursue him anytime soon, and by that time he'd be well ahead of them. Surely, after all this, they'd give up on their meaningless task of pursuit.

⌘

Chapter Four

Ft. Worth was just hitting its growth spurt in 1875 as Buck viewed it for the first time. Not a particularly big town to some, it looked like a big city to Buck. He'd heard talk of the gamblin' halls, the saloons and how Saturday nights were filled with partying, drinking, loud talk and occasional gunfire. It certainly didn't look that way as he rode in shortly before noon.

Buck first noticed the train station on the edge of town. It was a magnificent structure, amazingly different from the one in Corsicana. Trains had always fascinated him, so he stopped there first to watch as a narrow-gauge steamer rolled out of town. Blaze jumped noticeably as the engineer pulled the whistle to signal its departure, so much so that Buck had to grab the saddle horn to keep from falling off.

"Settle down Blaze," he said. "I know this is a big place, but them's the same whistles you've heard before in Corsicana."

Blaze settled down at once and Buck continued to gaze at the train until it was well out of sight. He heard it signal four more times, indicating road crossings. Buck imagined to himself how many streets this town must have, figuring that there were at least four on that side of town alone!

As he turned north on what appeared to be the town's main street, he next noticed two or three saloons, with no apparent activity at any of them. At this time of day that was understandable, but Buck imagined what they would be like in a few hours. Next he espied a general store, a boot store, a couple of lawyer's offices, a physician's establishment, and finally a livery stable.

"Man," Buck exclaimed. "I weren't prepared for somethin' like this." With that he dismounted and led Blaze over to the livery.

Buck walked into the stable and was met by a friendly, balding man that appeared to be in his forties. He was a good deal shorter than Buck, but from the looks of his arms and thick neck he had spent the biggest part of his life doing physical labor. This observance appealed to Buck for he had thought that he'd only meet up with "town" folk here.

"Howdy," the jolly man offered. "What can I do for you son?"

Buck immediately liked the tone of his voice. When the man called him "son" he meant no disrespect and Buck took no offense.

Buck responded promptly, "Guess you'd say I could use several things. I need feed, hay and water for my horse, Blaze. Also need some answers to a question or two."

"Well you've come to the right place, son," the man replied. "Ain't no charge for question answerin', but I'll have to be paid for takin' care of that fine lookin' piece of horse flesh," he continued with a chuckle.

"How much would you charge for takin' care of Blaze for the time bein'?" Buck asked.

"Well, I usually get a nickel for that kind of care, but you look like a young man who might be hard pressed to come up with that kind o' money, at least on a regular basis," the man offered. "What would you say to three cents? Could you go that?"

"Sure mister," Buck answered. "And I'm much obliged for your generosity."

"Glad to do it," he replied. "And you can call me Lyle. Most folks in these parts do."

Buck was amazed that he felt so good about having met this kindly man so soon after arriving in Ft. Worth. In his previous nineteen years you could count on one hand the number of folks who had this kind of effect on him. And to his surprise, he felt like he'd made a friend right there in the heart of the biggest town he'd ever been in.

Lyle went about his business while Buck removed saddle, bridle and blanket from Blaze. In a moment he questioned Buck. "Who are you, son, and where you come from?"

"Name's Buck Ward, and I hail from down around Corsicana," Buck responded. "Ever heard of it?"

"Sure, sure," he said. "Fact is, I met a man the other day from there. Rode in here with a young woman. They was having wheel trouble on their buckboard and I fixed it for 'em."

The moment Buck heard the word "woman" he grew tense and his face quickly changed color. "They say their names?" Buck asked, trying to hide his obvious interest.

"Let's see," the blacksmith answered. "My memory ain't what she used to be. Think it was Cobb, or was it Cole. That's right, it was Cole. Ned Cole. Don't recall hearing the young lady's name."

Buck turned red with anger when he heard the name Cole. He had fought the thought that he had come to Ft. Worth with the idea that he would confront Ned and Kelly. Now he knew for sure what he had been afraid of. He did come here for that, and his new friend's mention of the name set that straight. Only time would tell whether he'd be able to control his deep resentment and anger.

Something caused Buck to confide in Lyle. "I guess I'll spill the beans," he began. "Ned Cole and the girl, Kelly Stanfield, came from Corsicana all right. Fact is, Kelly was my girl. Then one day this dude Cole, fresh from somewhere back east, came to town and it was as if Kelly had never seen a man before. I told her he was no good from the start, and it weren't long before everyone in town knew it 'cept Kelly. He promised her this and that, and she fell right for it. Anyway, it weren't long before I knew I was up agin something that I didn't know how to handle. The next thing I knew, I went to call on her and she was gone, without even a word from her except what her sister told me. And that was only, "Goodbye."

"I knowed something about them two bothered you 'cause soon as I mentioned his name you got red in the face. Fact is, a look came to you that caused me to think you'd be one tough hombre to handle if'n you got mad. Now I know what caused that look," Lyle remarked.

"You got me pegged, Lyle," Buck responded with his eyes pointed to the ground and his hands deep in his pockets.

"Buck, awhile ago when you rode up you said you needed some answers to questions," Lyle offered. "You never got around to askin' them. I'll bet now one of them questions is what do I think you ought to do."

"Guess that's 'bout right," Buck answered. "I tried to fool myself all the way here that I was just going to ride a little out of my way to see a big town. Now I know that weren't true, but for the life of me I don't know what to do now."

Lyle thought for a moment as he scratched his baldhead. "Well, I'm not good at givin' love advice. Had my heart broke more'n once myself. But, by golly son, if I was you I'd look that feller Ned up and confront him hard about the subject. Then I'd look that girl in the eye and tell her just what you thought. You may never get over her if'n you don't."

"I 'spect you're right," Buck replied. "Guess that's what I'll do, but I think I'll wait a while before I do. For now though, I need to have those answers. First off, I need a place to stay a night or two. Got any suggestions?"

"Assumin' you don't mind sleepin' here in the stable, you can lay up right here," Lyle responded.

"That'd be right nice of you, Lyle," Buck responded. "That way I could keep a close eye on Blaze. Next question is where to get a good meal in this big place. I'm shore hungry."

"Ain't but one place I'd recommend," the blacksmith answered. "Right down the street on the right, place called Drummond's. Best food in these parts, and they don't take you to the bank on prices."

"Well I'll just git settled and then head on over there," Buck stated. "Wouldn't want to join me, would you?"

"Guess I better not," Lyle said. "My wife might git a little upset if I let her cookin' go to waste."

"Wife . . . you never mentioned a wife," Buck said in a surprised tone.

"Come to think of it I guess I never did," Lyle responded. "I got one of the best. Want you to meet her if you hang 'round long enough."

"You bet I will," Buck said. "Now, for that last question. Got any ideas where Cole and Kelly might be?"

Lyle responded quickly by saying, "Ain't got no idea, but I can put you on someone that'll know. She knows everything in this burg. But right now, go get that belly full and then have you a night out on the town. A handsome feller like you needs some fun now and then. We'll talk about that in the morning."

Buck walked away toward Drummond's without even responding, almost as if he was taking a direct order from Lyle. His mind wandered as he went about gazing at the Ft. Worth sights.

He first thought about his fortune of meetin' up with this kindly blacksmith. Of all the places in Ft. Worth he could have gone first, he came to this one. Lyle must have sensed that Buck needed a friend. Buck didn't know 'till now that he needed one so badly.

Next, he thought about Kelly, the only girl he ever had. He was still mad as a hornet at what had happened, yet for some reason it didn't seem to hurt so much now. Buck didn't know that the immediate friendship he'd struck up with Lyle probably accounted for the easing of the pain.

He espied Drummond's right where Lyle had told him it'd be. It was situated in between a dry goods store name Dillard's Mercantile and the undertaker's. Buck mused to himself that he guessed that if'n the food was so bad that it killed him they wouldn't have to drag him far to get him taken care of.

Drummond's was almost empty when Buck walked in. It was too early for most folks to be eating, but not for Buck. He liked to eat a hearty meal in the early afternoon and then just kinda snack later on. That kept him from going to bed feeling too full.

The surroundings were quite different than the place he ate at in back in Boyce. This place had some style to it. All the tables were round, indicating they could've been store bought. Each one had a white tablecloth on it, with plates and utensils already setting out on it. Right in the middle of every one was a jar with a flower or two sticking out of it. The walls in the place were painted white and there were pictures, nice pictures, hanging ever so often.

Buck gazed at one or two of them before he heard someone address him.

"Sir, do you care to be seated?" the voice said.

"Guess it's purty hard to eat standin' up," Buck joked as the young lady showed him to a chair.

The girl waiting on him couldn't have been more than twelve or thirteen years old. She was a cute girl, with bright red hair and freckles to match. She was dressed in a frilly dress with flowers all over it. Buck guessed that she might be related to the proprietor.

"Do you want something in particular, or do you want to see a menu?" the young girl asked.

Buck had never eaten in a place that had a menu before so he responded, "Let me see the menu."

Buck's book learning was mighty weak, and he wasn't ready for what was coming. The girl brought the menu and it was filled with fancy words, some in languages Buck couldn't recognize. He hoped the girl didn't notice his red face as he was trying to figure out what was on the menu.

"On second thought I'll just have a beefsteak, beans and coffee if'n you please," Buck stated.

"How do you want that steak cooked?" the waitress asked.

"Just right there in the skillet," Buck responded. It was obvious he had never been in a fancy place like this before.

"No sir," the girl said, trying to keep from laughing. "What I mean is, do you want it cooked lightly or do you want it left on for a while?"

"Whatever it takes to get it black on both sides is what I want," Buck answered with a slightly disturbed look on his face.

"Yes sir," the girl said as she walked away.

Buck began wondering what kind of place he'd come to. He'd never had so many decisions to make before in ordering a meal. He felt uncomfortable because he was afraid he'd mess something up there on the table. And to top it all off, he didn't know what to do with all the utensils setting before him on the white tablecloth.

He looked around to see if he could pick up any ideas from somebody else in the place. He noticed a young couple setting over on the far side of the room. They were seated across the table from each other and were involved in a conversation. They'd already finished their meal so they were no help. The only other folks in the place had their backs to Buck, so he couldn't see enough to help him out any.

Buck decided he'd just do the best he could, so he passed the time waiting on his meal by thinking about what he'd do and where he'd head after leaving Ft. Worth. He imagined that he'd head northwest from here, trying to stay away from Indian areas, and maybe try to catch on for a while at a ranch. He'd heard that there were some fine spreads between here and the Wichita Falls area. He also thought about doing some hunting along the way since deer and buffalo inhabited these areas in large numbers. In Corsicana, Buck was lucky to see one or two deer a year, and there were no big shaggies at all.

The young girl arrived with Buck's meal in less time than he thought it'd take. She placed it in front of him and asked, "Is there anything else I can get you, sir?"

"Guess not . . . looks fine to me," Buck answered. He began to dig in.

This might have been the best meal Buck had ever tasted. He thought about the many times he'd spent on the trail and had little or nothing to eat. Still, as good as it tasted and as nice as the surroundings were, Buck knew that town life was not for him. He longed for the open spaces and life on the trail.

Buck finished up his food and the young girl came to present his bill. When she handed it to him his eyes opened wide and his face showed an expression of complete shock. "Ma'am, you sure this ain't a mistake? This is more'n I paid for my last pair of boots, even if they were worn a little."

"No sir, " the girl replied. "That's the right amount."

Buck was about to get out the money to reluctantly pay when he heard some chuckling going on behind him. "Need a loan?" someone remarked.

Buck looked around to see Lyle standing there, laughing loudly at the predicament Buck was in. He was not used to being laughed at, and his face must have shown it.

"Settle down now Buck," Lyle offered as he grabbed Buck's shoulder and gave it a squeeze. "I set this whole thing up. You see, my wife runs this place and this here girl's my daughter, Sally. I snuck in after you got here and told the girls to do this. Thought it'd be a good trick to play on you after I told you the prices was reasonable." Lyle laughed again as he sat down beside Buck at the table.

"Well, you can bet your bottom dollar your trick worked," Buck responded. "I got a little money, but I knew it'd be gone fast in a town like this if them prices was the goin' rate."

Lyle went on to explain to Buck how he and his wife came to town quite a few years ago with nothin' in their pockets, but had worked hard to establish themselves. After the livery business got pretty good, they saved enough to buy the cafe. The rest was history.

"Now, Buck," he said, "Forget about that bill. It's on me. Git on out of here and git ready for your education on the nightlife here in Ft. Worth. And have a good time doin' it."

Grandpa stopped the story at that point and said, "I'm tired and that's enough for now. Let's get this table cleared, help your mother with the cleaning and get ready for bed."

Poppa joined in with other instructions and all of us kids knew it'd be no use to argue, no matter how interested we were in the story. We knew the best way to get on with it was to agree to do whatever they said and hope that Grandpa would be in a mood to continue tomorrow.

That night as I went to bed I lay awake dreamin' about Buck and his adventure. I wished that I could set out on a trek like Buck, but it wasn't the same in 1927 as it was then. Little did I know then, though, that a few years later I would go on an adventure like Buck, except it'd be by riding the rails west, as a honest-to-goodness hobo.

The next day all of us got a break and it rained all day long. Sittin' around the small house with nothin' much to do caused Grandpa to offer to continue with the story. Everyone was excited, even Poppa. I knew this when he said, "Well, you can't work all day long every day. Ya'll gather on around and let's get started."

I'd never before heard him back off much from his belief in hard work.

⌘

Chapter Five

By the time Buck walked out of Drummond's it was approaching five o'clock. It wouldn't be dark for a while longer, and Buck knew the town wouldn't really be waking up until then.

Buck had no intention of losing his head, getting drunk and waking up the next morning wondering what had happened the previous night. He had only tasted hard liquor a few times in his life, and he knew enough from those instances that he wasn't going to acquire a taste for it. He'd also seen enough of the effects of liquor on folks in his own family to know that he didn't need to take a chance on getting hooked on the stuff.

Nevertheless, Buck wanted to experience some of what he'd heard about down in Corsicana. So he planned on slipping in on a saloon or two, see if he could catch a glance at least one pretty girl, and maybe try his hand at a game or two of poker.

As he walked down one of the side streets looking at the sights, Buck thought again of Ned Cole and Kelly Stanfield. It was strange to him that he'd already lost some of the anger he had earlier in the day. Still, he wanted to see Kelly one last time, and he wanted to look Ned in the face and challenge him for what he'd done.

About that time he came up on a store with a glass front on it. In the window he saw the finest pair of boots he'd ever seen before. A big sign over the window displayed the name Marshall's Boot Makers.

Buck had never had a new pair of boots that he could remember, and it took him only one glance to pick out the pair he would purchase if he could afford them. They were chocolate in color, different from the usual black that most men wore. They had a high sloping heel on them that would enable a man to stick in the stirrups during the wildest ride. The toes were pointed, but it was the tops that particularly caught his eye. They had rows and rows of stitching, so many that he couldn't count them from where he was standing. The stitching formed a pattern that reminded him of an eagle flying free. The extreme tops of the boots were shaped like the upper portion of a heart, with holes on each side to put your fingers in. Buck had never seen anything but rounded tops before.

Buck unconsciously felt of the money belt under his coat as if to wonder if he could afford these magnificent boots. His common sense told him that he couldn't possibly afford them, but a strange side, one he'd maybe never before experienced, urged him to buy them. Luckily the store was closed, so any decision on this would have to be delayed.

Once he came back to reality, Buck noticed the sound of loud piano music coming from just up the street. Evidently the evening had begun, so he followed the sound until he came to some swinging doors. It was a good deal fancier than any saloon he'd been in before, but the sounds and the smoky atmosphere brought back memories of times past.

Buck waltzed through the door carefully to try to not create any special attention. The bar room was large, with many tables scattered around and three or four chairs positioned at each. On the side closest to the street Buck noticed an empty table, so he headed that way and settled himself quietly as he continued to take in the sights.

The bar in the establishment was long, perhaps 30 to 40 feet in length, with a short L- shaped part attaching to the far wall at one end. Shelves behind it were lined with so many bottles of drink that Buck thought there must not be any kind of liquor that the place didn't serve. A large mirror separated the shelves in the middle. Right in the center of this were big letters reading, "MAN WAS PUT HERE TO HAVE FUN. THIS PLACE WAS PUT HERE FOR MAN."

To the left of the bar, and extending at a right angle away from it, was a stage. It was decorated fancy-like. Buck had never seen such a stage before, but he imagined some of the dance hall girls he'd heard about performed on it. One thing he was sure of. He wanted to be there when and if they did.

The place was only about one-third full at this early hour, but the noise level was already beginning to rise. A painted lady dressed in a colorful outfit approached Buck about that time and asked him if he would buy her a drink. Buck thought about it a minute, quickly remembered being warned about this approach before, and politely told her he was waiting on someone else to join him. She left without appearing disturbed at all.

Buck looked over in one corner of the room and saw something that caught his eye. It was a table of gamblers, intent on their game. There were only three players so Buck imagined that they might accept him in if he asked. He first tried to inconspicuously retrieve a few dollars from his hidden belt, but this proved to be a trick in itself. However, he eventually got what he wanted, put it in his pants pocket, and walked slowly toward the table.

As he approached, a fancy eastern-type gentleman saw him coming and spoke first. "Looks like we may have another player, boys. Am I right mister?"

"I might be interested in sittin' in on a round or two," Buck answered. "What's the game?"

The easterner replied quickly, "Stud. And it's the fairest game you'll find in this one-horse town."

"Sounds good to me," Buck replied. "I'm in."

Sitting down Buck inspected the others around the table. The man immediately across from him was rough looking, with a scraggly beard and dark black hair hanging out from under his hat. His hair was obviously unkempt. Buck imagined that this man was probably down on his luck and was looking to the game to change that. To his left sat a huge man, dressed in a store-bought suit, with a half-smoked cigar dangling from his mouth. He seemed to be totally engrossed in the game, hardly even paying any attention to Buck. Next to him sat the easterner, who seemed to be able to talk enough for all of them.

"Where you hail from, cowboy?" asked the easterner.

"South of here a ways," Buck replied. "Just passin' through these parts."

"Well that's lucky for you," he replied back. "My luck's been bad, and you sure might be able to cash in on that."

Buck's natural distrust for men kicked in about then. Anytime someone told him he was about to come upon good fortune, he figured him to be lying. However, he coolly said, "Shore hope so."

Buck played three or four hands without winning or losing much. He quickly noticed that the cowboy had been drinking heavily and was impaired in his ability to play well. The big man was in over his head and continued to lose heavily, although his money supply was abundant enough for that not to stop him. The easterner, though, was slick in both his mental approach to the game and in the way he handled the cards. Buck decided to keep a close eye on him.

Two or three more hands were played before Buck hit a string of luck that resulted in his going up more than $25 to the good. During this part of the game several other folks in the saloon noticed his good fortune and began to gather around as they continued to play.

"You really know how to play this game," asserted the easterner. "I hope you give me a chance to win some of that back."

"Well, as a matter of fact," Buck began. "I think I've had just about enough."

Buck had been taught how to play poker while in the Civil War. He must have learned from some of the best, because he seemed to be able to hold his own with most anyone, even an occasional professional gambler like this easterner. He also learned when to leave, and he never deviated from what he'd been taught. Besides, that $25 would buy him that pair of boots in the window, and he didn't want to risk losing it.

"Can't believe you're leaving in the middle of a run like this," the gambler replied.

"Yeah, "remarked the big man. "Stay a while longer."

"Guess not," Buck said as he began to pick up his coins and stand up.

For a moment Buck thought he might have trouble from these three losers. However, he left the table without incident and they kept on playing after one of the onlookers took his place.

Buck walked back to the table where he was originally sitting and noticed that he'd left his hat there all the while. Two cowboys were now there, with two of the saloon girls sitting in their laps.

"Excuse me folks, but that's my hat there," Buck said. "Ill just get it and be outta y'all's way."

"Hold on there a minute, boy," one of the cowboys uttered as he winked at the painted lady sitting in his lap. "I think that there hat is mine."

Buck knew immediately that this situation could lead to trouble. He knew this type all too well, and to make matters worse, he noticed that both of the cowboys wore pistols on their hips.

"No mistake about it," Buck answered. "Fact is my name's written on the inside if'n you want to check."

"Don't need to check," replied the leader of the two. "I wore that hat in here and put it right down where it sits not more 'n an hour ago."

Buck surveyed the situation quickly and surmised that he was going to have to face these two in order to get his hat back. He smoothly moved his jacket to the side so that both cowboys could catch a glimpse of his Colt that they'd not noticed before. A definite change in their expressions resulted when he did this.

"Now I'm goin' to say it one more time. That's my hat, and I can prove it if'n it's necessary. Now hand it over or stand and let's get this over with quick."

Buck's coolness always seemed to give him an advantage over his opponents. And even though he wanted to avoid trouble, he couldn't let these two embarrass him in front of so many onlookers. In fact, Buck now realized that a pretty big crowd had gathered around.

The cowboy that did the talking rose slowly, tellin' the ladies to leave. He then said to Buck, "You're talking mighty big, especially for a boy that don't even got a holster."

"If you think you can beat me, I'll oblige you right now," Buck responded.

At that the second cowboy rose to face Buck head on. When this happened the crowd that had gathered around moved from behind him in anticipation of a gunfight.

"You think you can take both of us?" the cowboy asked.

"Only one way to find out," Buck said coolly. "Fact is, I've done it before, and against tougher hombres than you."

This cool defiance seemed to unnerve the two cowboys. They quickly glanced at each other, trying in some way to determine what the other was going to do.

Before they could decide Buck shouted to those gathered around, "Who runs this place?"

A lady spoke up quickly that said she was the manager and that they didn't want any trouble like this.

"I want you to witness this," Buck told her. "I don't want trouble either, but these cowboys want to steal my hat. Guess I'm gonna have to plug 'em for it."

"Drop them guns," a man yelled loudly from Buck's rear. "I got all of you covered."

Buck quickly glanced around to see a big man with a double-barreled shotgun pointed right at him. The man was obviously a lawman because he wore a badge high on the left side of his shirt. His demeanor was serious and Buck decided then that he'd better back off.

"Yes sir," Buck replied, quickly dropping his firearm.

The two cowboys were not so quick to oblige. The leader said, "Well, sheriff, it's a good thing you showed up when you did. We was about to have to kill this feller."

"Boys, did you hear me say drop them guns?" the sheriff replied. "Now let's get it done."

Both men then began to slowly unbuckle their belts and they dropped to the floor with a thud.

"Now tell me what this is all about," the sheriff demanded.

The cowboy who had spoke the least began first. "Sheriff, this here boy tried to steal my friend's hat. These ladies here can vouch for that," the man said as he pointed to the two girls who'd been sitting with them.

"That ain't exactly right," Buck offered. "I left that hat there when I went to play poker, and I can prove that it's mine. Just look on the inside and you'll see the name Buck written in it. That's me, sheriff. The name's Buck Ward."

The sheriff quickly grabbed the hat and checked Buck's story. "Looks like you were talkin' straight," the sheriff said. "But son, tell me, were you willin' to get killed over that hat?"

"Heck no, sheriff. I never thought about gettin' killed. Didn't figger these two could take me."

The crowd of onlookers who had gathered around started talking to each other in muffled voices. Most of the talk centered on the boldness of this tall Texan. Even though no gun was ever drawn, those who'd witnessed it figured that Buck would have come out on top. Fact is, the two smart-mouthed cowboys were lucky that the sheriff showed up when he did.

"You two misfits get outta here right now," the sheriff said in a demanding voice. "And I don't want to see you here again."

With that the two cowboys grabbed their belts and left.

"Mister Ward," the sheriff then said. "My advice to you is to keep that hat on your head from now on. Maybe it'll keep you from gettin' it shot off."

"I expect that's good advice," Buck responded. "And thanks, sheriff, for listenin' to my story."

Buck reached for the gun he'd dropped to the floor, tucked it safely into his belt, and headed for the door. Everyone in the place had their eyes on him.

"Not so fast there, son," the sheriff interrupted. "Might be good if I walked along with you for a spell. Them two fellers might just be waitin' for you down the street a ways."

"That's fine with me, "Buck responded. "Never had a bodyguard before."

The two men left the saloon and headed down the street. They were a forceful-looking pair as they walked side by side in the darkness. Both were tall and well built, with only the sheriff showing a slight sign of a middle-aged belly protruding over his belt. The sound of their boots on the wooden walkways echoed in unison for a few moments before the sheriff broke the silence of talk.

"Buck, I gotta say that was one of the coolest displays of raw courage I've seen," the sheriff said. "I figger you must have been in these tights before."

Buck thought a moment before responding. "Fact is, sheriff, I seem to run into trouble wherever I go. I just came to town to see the nightlife and to visit a couple of folks. I try to mind my own business, but somethin' always comes up to cause me problems. Just like tonight, somethin' little seems to grow into somethin' big."

"Know what you mean, son," the sheriff replied. "Was that way once for me before I pinned on the badge. Now my advice for you is to stay clear of burgs like Ft. Worth. Stay away from saloons and gamblin' halls as much as possible. Where you headed anyway?"

"West," Buck answered. "I'm headed for the high country in New Mexico territory. Been dreamin' of it for sometime now."

"Always wanted to go there myself sometime," replied the sheriff. "Never got a chance though. When you headin' out?"

"In a day or two," Buck answered. "First I want to look up two folks I used to know. You might know 'em.

Came here a short while back. Their names are Ned Cole and Kelly Stanfield, if'n they ain't been hitched up yet."

"Don't guess I know 'em, son," the sheriff said. "But good luck to you, and stay outta trouble."

The sheriff offered his hand and the two shook hands before the lawman turned and walked in the opposite direction.

Buck knew that the sheriff had saved him from having to shoot the two cowboys. He appreciated the intervention for Buck remembered all too clearly the feeling that came over him every time he had had to kill a man. It wasn't a good feeling, and sleep was hard to come by for quite a spell. Buck was simply a good-hearted cowboy who'd had a tough life, and there always seemed to be somebody around who wanted to make it tougher for him.

It was still only about 8 o'clock but Buck figured his nightlife was over. He walked back in the direction of the livery where he would spend the night when he thought about those boots again. He felt for the money belt and began to imagine how he'd look with them on. He then reasoned that the money he'd won in the card game was more than enough to buy them, and, after all, that money was some he'd not counted on having in the first place.

Buck wandered around for a while trying to find his way back to the livery. When he found his bearings he knew that he wanted to catch one last look at those boots before he went to sleep. The shop was dark inside, but the light of one of the many street lamps enabled him to catch a good look. They were as he remembered them. He decided then and there that he would buy them first thing in the morning.

As he walked away from the shop and headed for the livery he began thinking again about Kelly. He'd loved that girl, and she treated him badly. But he began to realize that he might be getting over her. Maybe it wasn't really love. After all, he'd never been in love before. Maybe he just thought he loved her. Anyway, in the short time since she had left, he felt that he could go on with his life. Still, he wanted to pay her one last visit before heading west.

The livery was dark as he entered, but he remembered a lantern hanging by the door and he quickly lit it so he could see to prepare his makeshift bed. He first walked over to Blaze and patted him on the rear and said, "Blaze ol' boy, if everything goes well tomorrow, we'll be headed west before noon. Would you like that, boy?"

Blaze didn't respond in any particular way but Buck imagined that he understood. He went on talking, "Yeah, Blaze, these big towns ain't no place for you and me. We need the open country where a man can see off. These buildings, the noise, the people...all spell trouble for us. No doubt about it, tomorrow we're gone."

Buck found his bedroll next to his saddle and quickly rolled it out in the stall alongside Blaze. He lay down, as always on his back, but this time only imagined that he could see the moon and the stars above. He told himself that tomorrow night would be different. After a brief time of reflection on the day's events, he told Blaze goodnight and fell asleep.

⌘

Chapter Six

Buck awoke to hear Lyle banging on an anvil just outside the livery door. He was singing a song Buck had heard before.

"All year o'er the prairies alone I do ride,
Not even a hound-dog to run at my side.
My fire I do kindle from chips gathered round
To boil up my coffee from beans that ain't ground.
My ceiling's the sky; my carpet's the grass
My music's the sound of the herds as they pass.
My books are the creeks, and my sermons the stones,
My parson's a wolf on a pulpit of bones."

He lay there on the straw for a few minutes thinking about the song and how it seemed to describe the life he was leading.

Loneliness was not something Buck feared. In fact, he preferred it, and his lack of material things was of no concern. Except those boots. . . he simply had to have those boots.

Buck got up quickly with three things stirring in his mind. First he wanted to buy the boots. Then he wanted to try to find Ned and Kelly. Finally, he wanted to get out of Ft. Worth and head toward New Mexico.

Using water from a horse trough near Blaze's stall, Buck shaved, slicked his hair back, threw on his hat, and snuck up on Lyle, still in the middle of singing that same song over again for the hundredth time. "Mornin'," Buck said as he approached Lyle. "I'm much obliged to you for lettin' me take a bed in the livery last night. I slept like a baby, and if it weren't for somebody singin' off tune I'd probably still be asleep."

Lyle responded as if he hadn't noticed Buck's last comment. "You're shore welcome Buck, my boy. Now

41

what does a young cowpoke like you have in store for a fine day like today?"

"Got lots to do," Buck responded with a sound of determination in his voice. "First off, I'm goin' to go buy me my first pair of store-bought boots. Then, I want to try to find those two no-goods from Corsicana and give them a piece of my mind. After that, I'm headed to the high country."

"Sounds like you been doin' some powerful thinkin' Buck. I hate to see you go so soon, son, just when I was takin' a likin' to you."

Buck pondered a moment on Lyle's words. It wasn't often that somebody told him they liked him. "In a way I hate to also," Buck finally responded. "But Lyle, I nearly got into a gun scrape last night. Think I'd better leave this town fast before trouble sets in."

"I understand, son," Lyle said. "Now let me give you a hand on one of them tasks. I asked around last night about your ol' girl and the easterner. Seems they been stayin' over at the Baskin Hotel for the last several days. This Ned feller has been gamblin' a lot at night and gets back in late. Your girl, Kelly, ain't been seen for quite sometime."

"Where's the hotel?" Buck asked with the intent of gettin' this business over with pronto.

"Go four streets down this way, turn right. You can't miss it. It'll be on your left-hand side not far from the corner," Lyle offered with his hand motioning in the right direction. "But son, don't go up there with fire in your eyes. Remember, you got lots of plans that jail won't set with right away."

"OK, Lyle," Buck answered. "I'll try to take it easy."

Buck began quickly walking, following the directions Lyle gave him. His mind drifted from one extreme to the other, first thinking of talking only coolly with the two, and then thinking of a confrontation that could leave Ned out cold. At this point, Buck really had no idea what he'd say when he caught up with the two.

He turned the last corner and saw the big Baskin sign over the older, deteriorating hotel. Buck quickly realized that the two must be down on their luck to be staying in a dump like this. "Serves them right," Buck thought as he approached the front door.

Buck climbed the three steps that led up to the entrance and he opened it slowly. He walked in and up to the counter where he saw no attendant in sight. Ringing the bell on the counter, Buck waited for somebody to respond. As he waited, his thoughts were of only one thing. He wanted to get this business over with and get out of there. In a way, he was feeling a little embarrassed that he'd gone to such lengths to confront the two.

After a few moments an older man with a graying beard and white hair stepped out of an adjoining hallway and responded to Buck's call. "What can I do for you mister?"

Buck responded immediately with, "I'm lookin' for Ned Cole. Is he stayin' here?"

"Shore is son," the man answered. "Number 7, up the stairs and to the right, last door on the right."

Buck was gone before the man finished his last directions. He climbed the stairs and entered a rather dark hallway with light coming from only a window at the end. It had some sort of covering over it, thus letting in only some of the morning's early sunlight. The numbers were painted on the dark doors, so Buck had to get close to each one before he could make them out. He finally found the one marked seven, took a deep breath to calm his nerves and banged loudly with his fist. No answer came, so he knocked again with more forcefulness.

Buck heard a mumble and some shuffling in the room. It was at that moment that he realized that he was probably doing one of the dumbest things he had ever done in his life. After all, here he was, knocking on the door of a man that he despised, and a girl who'd betrayed him. He didn't know if they'd been married, but if Kelly was in the room he was sure to embarrass her good, not to mention the way it'd affect him. Ned would probably be the only one not to be bothered by the confrontation. On top of all that, Buck didn't know, even now, what he'd say to the two of them if they answered.

A shout came from inside the room that was unmistakably Ned's. "What is it you want?"

"It's Buck Ward. I want to talk to you two."

Ned's response came angrily. "I ain't got no business with you, Buck. Now get out of here. It's too early in the morning to be arguing with you."

Buck's emotions had already built to the point that he wasn't interested in talking. He took Ned's response to be non-negotiable, so he promptly kicked the door soundly, causing it to crash open with a bang. He entered the small room to see Ned, only half dressed, standing beside the bed, quite startled at Buck's sudden entrance.

"You must be crazy!" Ned shouted as he maneuvered around the bed to face Buck head on. "What are you doing here?"

"I'm here to face you and Kelly straight up about the stunt you pulled. Where is she anyway?"

"Aw, that good for nothin' hussy left two days ago," Ned responded as redness entered his face for the first time.

Buck couldn't control the emotion that came over him when he heard those words. He stepped quickly toward Ned and swung his powerful fist before Ned realized what was coming. The blow landed smack on his nose. Blood began flowing freely as he rose from the position where he'd landed and Buck hit him again on the side of the face. This second blow ended the fight.

Ned was not unconscious, but was beaten badly. He was lying on the floor beside the bed when Buck spoke. "Now, you two-bit easterner, I wanna know what happened to Kelly, and don't you gamble and call her a hussy again."

"All right," Ned responded, trying to clear his nose of the blood that was still flowing. "Just don't hit me again and I'll tell you all of it. Here's what happened. While we were in Corsicana I kept telling Kelly that she should get out of that no-good town and go with me to a real town. I told her about Ft. Worth, and all the exciting things that could happen to her here. Finally, I told her that she needed to make up her mind because I was leaving the next morning. She finally agreed to come, and we set out in the buckboard. She started whining about making the wrong decision almost before we got out of sight. We argued a lot, and I kept telling her that things would get better. It didn't, and to be honest, she kept talking about you, Buck. I got fed up with it and told her to hit the trail. She walked out two days ago, and I don't know where she went.

"One more question," Buck responded. "Did you promise to marry her before you left Corsicana?"

"Yeah, I'll admit I did," Ned answered. "But I never really aimed to."

"And did you violate her in any way?"

"No. Fact is, she never let me touch her," Ned responded.

"Well it's a good thing you didn't. No tellin' what I'd do to you right now if'n you had," Buck said with a tone of anger in his voice. "As it is, I hope our paths never cross again."

Buck left the room with many thoughts in his mind. He had to go somewhere and think, and he did his best thinking on the trail. He'd had enough of the big town life. He had to get away and he had to do it quick.

He walked the few streets back over to the livery and began making preparations for his departure. Lyle wasn't around, so he left two bits on the makeshift desk in the corner, rolled up his few belongings that were still in the stall where he slept, saddled up Blaze and quickly led him down the street. It was then and only then that he thought about the boots that he wanted so badly, yet he didn't want to turn back now. He mounted, softly spoke a word to Blaze and set off on his trek west.

⌘

Chapter Seven

It was close to eight o'clock when Buck reached the edge of town and he could look west without seeing any sign of civilization. This country was already different than the land he'd left. The soil was reddish in color. The terrain had become rocky in places. Large live oak trees frequented the landscape, and there were gentle rolling hills to cross. He could see in the distance some hillsides that seemed to contain nothing but grass. Then, to each side of these, he could see places that didn't seem to resemble those at all.

Buck found that his departure had him thinking of Kelly more than of the trek he was setting out on. Evidently, she did love him. And when he heard Ned speak of this, he knew that he loved her, too. But why had she deserted him that way? Didn't she know that his pride was too great to take her back now? And where did she go when she left Ft. Worth? He assumed that she would make her way back to Corsicana, a place Buck now was uncertain that he'd ever visit again.

As he tried to put Kelly out of his mind he realized that he'd left town without thanking Lyle for his help. He realized that Lyle had befriended him at a time when he was desperate for friendship. He'd offered counsel and advice that proved to be right on target. He'd joked with him, poked fun at him, and even helped him financially. It was hard for him to imagine that all this had taken place in less than two days.

Buck thought once about turning back and giving Lyle the good-bye that he deserved. Then he thought that it might be better to write him a letter. He'd be more likely to say the right thing by doing this, even if his grammar and punctuation might leave something to be desired.

His next thoughts were of those boots he'd longed for. Next to feeling bad about leaving without saying bye to

Lyle, his biggest regret of his quick departure was leaving those boots in that window. Why hadn't he stopped to get them? Was it anger? Was it pride? He searched for the answer but didn't come up with a suitable one.

With all that was on his mind, Buck realized that he'd not been paying attention to Blaze on this first day away from Ft. Worth. He quickly spoke, saying, "Blaze ol' boy, it's you and me now. I know for sure you'll never let me down, will you boy?"

Buck knew the answer in his heart. Blaze was a friend for life, and perhaps the only one he'd have for quite sometime. And at this moment in Buck's life, that's exactly the way he wanted it.

After three or four hours of easy riding, Buck came up on a creek bed that offered a nice place to take a rest. He really wasn't hungry, for some reason, so he just loosened the saddle and let Blaze eat some of the winter grass that lined the banks. There was a small pool of water for Blaze to drink from, but most of the creek was dry, even in this wet part of the year. Buck imagined that it wouldn't be long before the water would completely dry up.

Thinking about the later summer months caused Buck to begin making plans for this long journey west. In a way, Buck felt that he had only begun the trip since he left Ft. Worth; for it was there that he'd heard the statement that the west only begins when you leave Ft. Worth. He now had to begin thinking about what route he'd take up to the panhandle and over to the border. He needed to determine where his stops would be, what food and belongings he'd need and where Blaze would need tended to. Because of the threat of Comanches he needed to know how to avoid them the best he could. Occasional jobs had to be taken in order to keep enough money to negotiate the full trip. "Man," he thought. "I should have thought about some of this before now. I'll bet ol' Lyle could have headed me in the right direction."

When he thought of Lyle he once again felt badly about his quick departure. He decided to attempt to write him a letter right then and there so that he could mail it at the next town he came to.

Buck got up from the place he was sitting and walked over to Blaze who had moved about thirty yards away in his quest for good eating. "Blaze," he said. "Hold still a minute so I can get to them saddle bags. I got a tablet and lead in there somewhere, and I need it right now."

Blaze stood still just as if he knew every word Buck said. Buck found the writing materials buried at the bottom of the bags and tried to straighten the wrinkles out of the paper as he returned to the spot where he was previously sitting.

It was about noon now, but Buck still didn't feel hungry, so he set about writing the letter, oblivious to the nature that surrounded him.

Dear Lyle,

I'm settin on a creek bank somewhere west of Ft. Worth and thinkin about all that happened to me the last two days. Fore I forgit, your friendship means a lot to me and I'm downright ashamed to have left without sayin anything. Hope you found the money I left for Blaze and my bord.

I want you to know that I found Ned Cole in that dump of a hotel you told me about. He didn't want to talk so I kicked the door in and caught him tryin to get his britches on. Kelly weren't there. Ned said Kelly had left two days before and he didn't know where she went. I ruffed him up purty good and he finlly told me that he near forced her to go with him and that she never really wanted to go. Said she talked about me all the time. He ended by tellin me that he never forced hisself on her.

Lyle, I realized for sure that I loved that girl when he talked bad about her. I figgered out that she must love me too cause she talked about me so much. If things were diffrent I'd go after her. Guess I'm too stubborn now to make that move.

*Well, now I'm headed for the high countrie. Wish I'd
done more checkin on the route to take and where I might
catch on for a while. This countrie's a lot diffrent from
Corsicana, or even Ft. Worth for that matter. I'll try to
steer clear of Comanchies and any other trouble for a
while. Thought I might catch on at the Waggoner, but I've
alredy decided to go further before stayin on somewhere.*

*I'll try to write again ever once in a while. I'll be
makin a line for Young Territory in the panhandle now.*

Your Friend,

Buck Ward

*P.S. Lyle, I hate that I didn't buy them boots, the
chocolate ones with lots of stitchin. I'm afraid I'll have
them on my mind for some time now.*

By the time Buck finished the letter it was about one
o'clock and he still hadn't eaten anything. He set about to
rustle something up when he caught his first glimpse of a
wild turkey in these parts. Over in Corsicana turkeys were
almost never seen, and he got a thrill at this first sighting.
And that's all he got, because the gobbler ran into the brush
almost as soon as Buck saw him.

He finished eating within thirty minutes, whistled for
Blaze to come and set out again. The sun was high
overhead now, and was quite hot for a spring day. There
was no wind rustling and he was still dressed for harsher
weather. He knew that it wouldn't be long before he'd have
to shed some of the warm garments he'd brought for those
that were designed for Texas summers.

Blaze quickly got into one of his slow, but steady gaits
and Buck's mind began to map out his trek to the New
Mexico territory.

First he thought about how long the trip might take. It
was probably more than 600 miles from here to Las Vegas,
the largest town on the eastern slopes of the northern New

Mexico Rockies. On a good day he might be able to travel fifty or sixty miles. If a man factored in all the things that could cause him to have to slow down, it probably wasn't realistic to expect more than 20 miles a day on the average. Then, figuring that he'd have to take a job here and there to make some wages and to avoid spending his entire stash, he was certain that it might take him at least two months. That is, if he didn't have any problems with the Comanches.

The Comanches roamed all of the southern plains in those days. They were among the most feared of Indian tribes, and were known to show no mercy in their confrontations with their white-faced intruders. Even though many were now located on a reservation arranged by a treaty signed in 1867, there were sufficient numbers left to spark fear in most folk's eyes.

Buck had heard some terrifying stories about how the Comanches tortured their captives. But what impressed him most was how they were known to be the best horsemen who had ever lived. Stories of how they'd ride bareback at full speed and fight or shoot buffalo were abundant. They were known to slide down to the side of their mounts during confrontations so they could avoid the enemy's shots. They revered their horses almost as much as life itself. This caused Buck to respect them more than most white folks of that day. Still, he was not looking forward to meeting one out in this wide-open country.

Thinking of the Comanches and their quest for buffalo caused Buck to become excited about seeing a buffalo for the first time. He'd heard and read about the big shaggies, as they were called. Much bigger than cattle, buffalo roamed the ranges in those days by the thousands. They were so thick that more than 200,000 hides had been sold in Ft. Worth alone earlier in that year during a two-day sale. They were unintelligent animals, and this, combined with their bulkiness, caused them to be easy prey for hunters and poachers alike. Buck had no way of knowing at the time that within a matter of ten years or so, the buffalo would be gone from the plains, a victim of the white man's greed.

Sure that he'd get to see more than one herd before long, Buck then began to dream about New Mexico. He'd first been told about the area where he was heading by a private he knew during the war. The boy was from that part of the country and he couldn't stop talking about it. In fact, Buck got fed up with it one day and told the private that he'd better stop the talk before he got mad enough to take matters into his own hands. The boy quit after this encounter, but Buck's curiosity got the best of him and he started quizzing him about why he liked it so much. What the boy said always stuck in his mind.

"Buck," he said. "The New Mexico Territory ain't like nothin' you ever seen there in Texas. Aw, sure it's got the barren plains, cactus and dust like Texas. But when you get to the mountains, everthin' changes. In the heat of the summertime, you don't even work up a sweat there. When you take a deep breath you feel like you're on top of the world. And, believe it or not, you almost are, cause them mountains are high, higher than you can see. There's wildlife abundant for the takin', and the mountain streams are so full of fish that they just invite you to bring 'em in. The winters are cold, but you've never seen nothin' more beautiful than mountains capped with white snow. Land's free for the takin'. I had a pard who said that a man would be a fool to live anywhere else but in the New Mexico Territory. And Buck," he said. "I ain't no fool."

Those words had a big impact on Buck. He'd never seen snow, couldn't imagine a place that was cool all the time, and the thought of fish and wildlife everywhere simply excited him. On that very day, Buck set his sights on going to those mountains.

Up ahead Buck noticed a slight change in the scenery. It was almost as if he was experiencing something twice in one day. Here, just like it did outside of Ft. Worth, the terrain changed again to flat prairie. These changes seemed to endear Buck to the land. He liked the variations, sometimes hilly, with grassy meadows and live oaks. At other times, he'd see the flattest land you could imagine.

51

Buck had traveled for two or three hours since his last stop there on the creek bank when he was startled to see something move off to his right. He estimated that it must be approaching six o'clock by the position of the sun in the sky, just the right time to expect to see a whitetail buck like this one. He briefly caught a glimpse of a nice set of antlers as the big boy disappeared into a thicket of mesquites.

Buck had seen many deer before, and had killed a few in his time. However, he'd never had an opportunity to get a shot at one as big as this one, so he thought he'd take a stab at trailing him. He quickly pulled Blaze to a halt and spoke ever so softly to him. "Blaze, let's call it a day." With that, he pulled the bridle off, loosened and removed the saddle, and let him go on his own.

From the saddle scabbard Buck removed the Model '73 Winchester lever action rifle he was carrying. It was the identical caliber of his pistol, a 44-40. This enabled him to be able to use the same ammunition in both, quite an advantage for a cowboy in those days.

The deer had not appeared unusually frightened when Buck last saw him. He'd heard enough tales about how to hunt deer that he knew that his odds of getting this one were slim, yet something told him to give it a try.

Buck slipped quietly into the cover where he saw the deer disappear. He began looking for any sign of a trail, but couldn't make out anything. It was grassy under the mesquites, and there were no evident signs that this was a common trail taken by deer or other wildlife.

Despite this, Buck continued quietly, taking only two or three steps at a time, then stopping for a few seconds to survey the outlying area. After ten or fifteen minutes passed, it began getting darker and Buck thought about turning back. He sure didn't want to get lost in the dark in a place he'd never been to before. But something made him continue on, just a few steps more.

Buck's keen eyes spotted the deer just ahead a little and to his right. It was positioned with its rear toward Buck, but its head was turned completely around so that it could keep an eye on him. The deer was probably no more than thirty yards away, but there was quite a bit of brush between it and Buck, so much so that Buck couldn't get a clear shot that he knew would drop it on the spot.

The deer stood perfectly still, as did Buck. Buck imagined that the deer might think that it was hidden from him, for what other reason was there for it to stand motionless such a short distance away? Maybe the deer had never heard gunfire, but that wasn't likely. This area had been the scene of heated Indian battles and buffalo hunts for years. Maybe it thought that Buck was not really a danger. But it had seen Buck follow its steps to this place. Maybe it was going to use its grace and speed to elude danger when and if it came. Buck really didn't know.

He felt he had to make a decision about what to do pretty soon because either the deer was going to bolt and run, or it was going to get too dark to see to shoot. With this thought Buck slowly moved to his right about three steps. Each step he took he tried to be as quiet and deliberate as possible, and he kept his eyes on the deer at the same time. He thought that if he took just two more steps that he could get a clear shot. In fact, he could almost smell that fresh venison in his frying pan already.

Then it happened. With his very next step he was scared plumb out of his wits. He'd stepped right into a covey of quail. When they flushed they made such a noise that Buck jumped away quickly, hit his head on a lower branch of a mesquite, and barely managed to keep the '73 in his hand as he tumbled to the ground.

His first thought was that he was glad no one was there to see him pull this stunt. Imagine, the cool, calm gunfighter Buck Ward, scared out of his mind by a bunch of birds! And to top it all off, Buck glanced toward the spot where the deer was standing and there was nothing there. Buck figured that the big buck must've thought it'd better vamoose soon before this clumsy cowboy hurt somebody!

Buck gathered his composure and turned to make his way back to where he'd left Blaze. As he went he could think only of what could or should have been. Why, if he'd shot when he first spotted the deer he might have been dressing him now. Or, even if he'd missed because of the brush he might have got a second shot at him with the lever action that he was so good with. Heck, he might not even get another chance at one of these wary animals. He was thoroughly frustrated.

He didn't have any trouble making his way back and finding Blaze grazing in the twilight of the moon that had just peeked out. He set about doing routine camp chores, gathering wood, preparing his bedroll to be used later, and making preparations for cooking some grub to eat.

Buck got his coffee brewing first and fried up some of the salt pork he'd brought. Salt pork and corndodgers sounded good to him, and so did the thought of being back on the trail again. He ate slowly, thinking all the time about his situation and coming back again and again to thoughts of Kelly.

His reminiscence caused him to remember back to the first time they'd met. Kelly moved to Corsicana from out east about seven years ago. Buck didn't meet her for a while after she came, but he remembered vividly that first meeting. He was eighteen and she was a year younger. She was sitting in the back of a wagon on the way to town when he first saw her. Her hair was curly and black as pitch. She wore it hanging down past her shoulders, and she had a habit of turning her head quickly to one side or the other to keep it from getting in her eyes. She also had the prettiest smile of any girl in the county.

That first day Buck couldn't help himself. He rode his pony right up behind Mr. Stanfield's wagon and boldly introduced himself. This was entirely out of character for Buck. Normally he was so shy that he wouldn't even think of talking to a stranger, much less a young girl.

"Howdy," Buck had said. "I'm Jeremy Ward, but most folks in these parts call me Buck. Are you new to this area?"

Kelly didn't answer at first, causing Buck to begin to be embarrassed at his unusual aggressiveness. Then she spoke. "Well, hello, Jeremy Ward. Nice to meet you, and my family's been in Corsicana now for about two or three months. Where have you been all that time?"

Buck remembered being so shocked that a girl of Kelly's age would be so forward, and right there with her parents in hearing distance. It caused him to mumble something and then to ride off in the opposite direction, without even really saying goodbye.

It was probably more than two weeks before Buck saw her again, but he'd been thinking about her all that time. He rode into town one day and saw her waiting outside Hank's general store. He got up enough nerve to go talk to her and it seemed that from that day forward the two developed a bond that was something he'd never had before, especially with a girl.

It wasn't long before he started calling on her. They would go for rides at first. Kelly liked riding almost as much as Buck did. And she could ride better than any female in those parts. She would ride astride her mount, unlike many girls of those days who rode only sidesaddle. Her favorite horse was a big grey that could run with the wind. It could easily outdistance Buck's horse of the time, a straggly sorrel gelding he had named Outlaw. She would kid Buck at every opportunity about this fact. Once she had said, "Jeremy, you look so funny way back there riding in my dust. You might as well get off and race me on foot!"

Buck could not remember a time when Kelly did not call him Jeremy. In fact, she was the only person he allowed to call him that. He never knew why, but he just never liked the name, except when Kelly called him that. It was somehow different with her.

Buck finished up his meal and scoured his skillet with sand because there was no fresh water available. When this was completed he stretched out on his back to look at the stars and to dream about the days to come. As usual, he fell asleep in just a few minutes.

Everyone in our family was disappointed when Grandpa looked at his pocket watch and said, "That's enough now. The rain's stopped, and there are chores that need to be done."

I didn't argue with Grandpa when he stopped, but the story about Buck Ward continued on in my mind. I would have given anything to have lived back in those days, when cowboys rode the range, drove cattle on the great trails like the Chisholm or the Goodnight-Loving, carried their six-guns and didn't seem to worry about where their next meal was coming from.

I quickly tended to the few chores that were assigned to me. I knew that they still took it easy on me, I guess because I was the youngest boy. When finished, I saddled up Roxie, got my favorite lariat rope and headed for the north pasture.

Using a rope was a fascinating thing to me. I'd seen Tom Mix a few months before in one of his local shows, and he could handle a rope better than anyone I'd seen. Lots of folks could throw a rope, but Tom Mix could spin and throw both. I was determined to be able to do the same, and I spent as much time as I could practicing. Sometimes I practiced so long that my arms would ache. It was worth it though, because I not only learned it, I used the skill to entertain others for many years thereafter. In fact, I was still spinning a rope when many of the boys I grew up with were dead and gone.

After a couple of hours of rope practice I mounted Roxie again and headed back to the house. As usual, I knew right away that I was in trouble again, but I didn't know what for.

"Travis Samuel, you get right in here in a hurry," Mama said with a definite anger in her voice. "Where have you been all this time, anyway?"

"Roxie and I've been out working on our roping, Ma," I replied trying to get on her good side. "Won't be long before I'll be bringing in money for my tricks, just like Tom Mix."

"Always talking about roping. Don't you ever get tired of that nonsense?" she demanded.

"Ma, you know it's not nonsense. Why, I'll bet Tom's made enough money doin' it that he won't ever have to work, I mean really work, for a living."

I could tell my efforts to get Ma's mind off what she was mad about wasn't working.

"Had a visitor while you were gone," she said. "Yeah, the school marm came by."

Those words froze me in my tracks. I knew that nothing she could have said would have been for the good, so I just braced myself for what was coming.

"Seems Miss Murdock is having a time getting you to pay attention in class. Says you've always got your mind on other things. Got any explanation for that?"

"Aw, Ma, it ain't always like that. I'll admit that sometimes I am thinking about ridin' or ropin' or the like. But you know, just a day or two ago I got the highest score in the class on my spellin' paper. Did she tell you that?"

"As a matter of fact she did," Mama answered. "That's just the problem she brought up. Said you were one of her brightest students, that is when you act like a student."

"Well Ma," I started. "It seems like every time . . ."

She cut me off short. "Don't start making excuses. Just start applying yourself to your work. And I don't want any back talk."

"Yes, ma'am," I said as I walked slowly to the room where me and my brothers stayed.

That night after supper we talked Grandpa into beginning the story again. I couldn't wait to hear more about Buck and his trip west.

⌘

Chapter Eight

Buck awakened earlier the next morning than normal. He figured the excitement of being on the trail again was the reason, but whatever it was, it afforded him the opportunity to be on the Texas prairie as the sun was just rising.

Nature had always had a special appeal to Buck. The beauty of it all confounded him, and he found himself always wanting to see more of it. That urge contributed to his call west.

Buck liked to look closely at the objects of nature. He'd look at flowers so closely that he could tell others of their most detailed parts. He knew the name of almost every tree that was grown in Texas. Animals were amazing to him, whether it be a small prairie dog which he was seeing quite a few of now, or the occasional smallish black bear he'd seen to the east during the war. The sky, the stars, the moon and yes, even the sun held special meaning to him.

This morning's sunrise was no exception. As he turned in the saddle and looked back to the east, he felt a sense of awe as he saw the brightness of it.

"Blaze," he said. "Have you ever thought about how that big ball got up there?"

Of course, no answer came from Blaze, but the question itself caused Buck to move to a deeper type of thought. Deep in his heart Buck had a sense of belief that there was a Creator out there somewhere. He'd been to church in Corsicana a few times, most recently with Kelly and her family. But the thought of there being someone, or something, out there in the heavens who spoke all of this into being, and then oversaw all of what transpired thereafter was difficult to comprehend. Surely there was some other explanation for creation and all that was in it. Then again, what explanation could mortal man come up with that would explain it all?

His quest to search for the answers to these questions had led him to reading the Bible that he carried in his saddlebags. Oh, he didn't necessarily do it on a regular basis, but when time and circumstances permitted, he would delve into its mysterious contents.

Of particular interest to him, other than the creation accounts in the very first parts, were the parts where this man Jesus appeared. Something within Buck longed to know more about him and his teachings. Yet Buck couldn't seem to comprehend the fact that someone as good as Jesus could really love a person who'd done so many wrong things as he had done. After all, he'd killed men who'd supposedly been created by this God. How could he take the first step toward God when he'd caused so many to never be able to approach him?

"Blaze, I got to get my mind on somethin' else," he remarked as they continued to ride along there on the Texas plains. "After all, I figger I'll always be at least one step from glory."

Buck continued to move in the general direction of Young territory for several more days.

More and more he was concerned with Indians, yet he'd been able to finally get that first deer, and he added a couple of turkeys along the way. "Man," he thought one day. "If I didn't have to worry about them renegades I could really make ends meet out here in this wilderness."

He'd hardly lost that thought when he noticed two riders in the distance to his right. They were probably four or five hundred yards away, but he could tell by the way they rode that they weren't white men. As they drew a little closer he knew they were Comanche, and he knew he'd better make some quick plans before they spotted him.

Buck quickly dismounted and drew Blaze in as close to him as he could as the both of them hid in a small clump of mesquites. He pulled on Blaze's reins so that his head didn't stick out over the top of the prickly branches of the closest one. Blaze didn't particularly like this treatment, but some easy coaxing reassured him enough that he kept quiet.

As Buck peered through the slight opening between him and the Indians, a cold realization hit him. He knew now that the Indians must have spotted him because they had now split up. One was riding directly at him at a slow but steady pace. The other was now circling to his right, toward the east, so that Buck had to look into the bright sunlight to watch him. He was riding at a considerably faster pace than the other one.

Buck had to come up with a plan fast, or he'd be forever lost on the prairie, with his bones being the only testament to his short life as a cowboy. He figured that he had two choices. He could jump on Blaze now and hightail it to the west. His mount was surely superior to the straggly Indian ponies the two Comanches rode. If there were no others out there he'd more than likely be able to escape the trap. On the other hand, Buck was confident that his prowess with a rifle would enable him to shoot the Indian coming at him from a considerable distance, and then he could take the other one on in a head to head confrontation.

Whatever plan he was going to choose he had to do it now. The first Indian was now only 150 yards away and the other was out of sight.

Buck talked quietly to Blaze to assure him that he knew what he was doing as he quickly drew out the '73 from its holster. The Comanche was now within a hundred yards and Buck could see him good. He noticed the man's sleek, slightly muscular build as he rode. He had long, flowing, jet-black hair that shined in the sunlight, and his face was marked with some sort of paint. He was carrying a rifle in his right hand, and his left was free. Yes, the Indian was riding and maintaining his balance simply by squeezing his legs tightly against the skinny pony.

Buck had never before shot at a human being without first having been either called out or shot at first. So as he raised the Winchester and pointed it at the oncoming Indian he was reluctant to shoot. However, at about that same moment he heard a shot from his right and felt the whizzing of a bullet go by that was too close for comfort. He knew then that he'd waited too long to make up his mind and now he was in a real fix. As he turned his eyes back to see the original Indian, all he saw was the paint pony standing about 75 yards away. . . by himself!

Buck had never been in this kind of predicament before. Here he was, stuck between two renegades, and he now had no idea where either one of them was. Yet his survival instincts began to kick in and the coolness that he was known for prevailed. And just in time too.

He took off in a dead run as fast as he could for the isolated pony. Buck was gambling that the rider had circled to the west after dismounting, hoping to catch Buck between him and his partner. His hunch was right because a shot was fired almost as soon as he took off, directly to his left. The shot was slow though, because he heard it hit slightly behind him and to his right. He was certain he'd caught both of his attackers off guard by moving in the direction from where they came.

Buck continued to run for at least fifty more yards, with two or three more shots falling harmlessly behind him. After he'd made this successful escape for the time being, he angled off to his right and into a gulch that he'd crossed only minutes before. Once in there Buck figured that he would be able to move more freely, and without being seen. The major problem now was that the Indians knew where he was and he now had no idea where they were. What a predicament!

Buck saw a big sandstone rock just a little way down the draw from where he entered it. He headed straight for it and dove to a safe position behind it as soon as he got there. The red West Texas sand covered his face as he slid to a halt, and he took a moment to clear his eyes as he secured the Winchester. He felt, almost subconsciously, for the Colt in his belt to make sure it was still there. In these close quarters the Colt might prove to be the weapon of choice.

The two Indians had been momentarily outfoxed by Buck's maneuver. However, now that he was in the draw, Buck realized that he was at a distinct disadvantage. Not only did they know where he was, they could cover the draw from on top without having much fear that Buck could see them. This disconcerted Buck. He knew he had to turn this disadvantage around, and fast.

He decided to follow his last strategy and make a move for different ground on the run. His strength and stamina were now real assets for him, and his ability to run fast came in real handy. He set out in the same direction as he had headed when he entered the draw. Running with boots and carrying a heavy rifle slowed him down some, but he heard no shots during the trek. As he ran, he tried to notice anything of significance that he might be able to use to his advantage. He passed several side draws and noticed two or three larger trees on the rim of the draw, but never saw anything that he thought could immediately help him out. By now his endurance was really being tested and he knew he'd have to stop for a blow shortly.

About that time Buck got the break that he needed. Up ahead, scarcely fifty yards away, he saw one of the Indians cross the gully he was in. Evidently the two had separated when Buck entered the draw, with one heading in one direction and the other going in the direction Buck chose. In this way they figured that one of them would find him. This, though, enabled Buck to be isolated with the one young brave he'd just seen, and now Buck knew where he was without being noticed.

He set out in the direction where he saw the brave with his pistol now in hand. After traveling about half the distance to where he saw him, Buck slowly crawled up the bank of the draw, a distance of about fifteen or twenty feet. He removed his hat and glanced over the rim, prepared to shoot at any time.

He was in luck. Just as he peered over the edge he saw the Indian through some mesquites heading back toward where Buck had just been. He obviously thought that he'd crossed the ravine far enough ahead of Buck to be unnoticed. That's were he was wrong, dead wrong. Buck picked out an opening where he anticipated the Indian to move through and prepared for a shot with the six-shooter. When he appeared Buck's training with a gun paid off. One shot stopped the warrior in his tracks.

Now Buck's thoughts had to turn to the other Indian. If his hunch were right, the other one would be well away now, still trying to find him in the opposite direction. The gunshot would certainly turn him around, and Buck meant to be ready when he did approach.

Buck decided to top the rim of the draw and move in a direction away from where he'd been. He hoped to get far enough away to find a suitable hiding spot where he could safely watch for the Indian's approach. If he could do this, he figured that he'd now have the upper hand on the Indian.

Buck tried to breathe as quietly as possible as he watched the terrain in front of him. He sat there in a crouched position for probably twenty minutes or more, his eyes steadily covering the area ahead. He thought his backside was safe, but then he started wondering what was taking so long for the Indian to appear. It was at that instant that he knew he was in trouble.

"Aiyeeeee!" came a blood-curdling scream from behind him. As Buck turned to respond he felt the cold blade of the warrior's knife whiff by his shoulder, barely missing its target. Buck responded by rolling to his side and coming up on his feet, now facing the Indian head on. He reached for the gun in his belt immediately, but before he could get it out the Indian charged, knocking it from Buck's hand. Now it was just Buck and the Indian, and the Indian still clutched the knife in his hand.

The two volleyed for position for a few moments, with the Indian swinging the knife toward Buck on several occasions. These swipes at Buck brought no results because each time he was able to maneuver away, just out of reach of the attacker.

Buck was all the while sizing up his adversary. The young Indian couldn't have been more than a teenager himself. Yet he had fire in his eyes, the eyes of a killer. Buck knew that there would be no stopping him short of death itself. It was the Comanche way, and although he'd never faced one in a battle like this, he'd seen the same look in men's eyes during the war.

Buck also knew that the Indian would be no match for him if he could avoid the knife. He was much bigger than the Indian, and his strength could be used to his advantage if he could get into a hand-to-hand battle.

The Indian let out another yell about that time and lunged at Buck with the knife pointed forward. Buck quickly stepped aside and took advantage of the move by grabbing the Indian's arm as it went by. He used all his strength to then draw the renegade's arm down and was able to get his other hand on the same arm. His strength paid off, because Buck's strong grasp caused the knife to be dislodged for the time being.

Buck knew then that the fight was as good as over. No man he'd ever met could match him in a fight like this, and surely this skinny redskin was no exception. Buck relentlessly hit the Indian three or four times, causing blood to appear about the Indian's eyes and mouth. On the last punch the renegade stayed down, almost knocked unconscious from the severity of the blow. However, he had just enough strength to lunge one last time for the knife lying in the sand. Buck saw this however, and beat him to it. As he raised the knife the Indian again charged, and Buck met him with the knife outstretched. As it penetrated the brave's body he yelled one last time, muttering something in the Comanche language that Buck surely didn't understand. Then he laid down, face first, in the West Texas sand, never again to raise a hand against a white man.

Buck felt no different after killing these two Indians than he had the times before when he'd had to kill men. There was no pleasure in it. Rather, he felt guilty and almost sick to his stomach. He stood there for a moment thinking that the taking of a life was such a waste. Why did it have to come to this? Why couldn't men of all kinds seem to get along? Why did it seem to always come down to his life or someone else's? Of course, Buck didn't come up with an answer to these questions, but they always haunted him.

⌘

Chapter Nine

The terrain grew more and more desolate as Buck and his mount continued traveling to the northwest for several more days. Eventually the plains leveled out to where he hardly ever saw any significant hills or valleys. Some called this area the Staked Plains. Others used the term Llano Estacado, which meant the same thing.

His first sighting of a big buffalo heard caught Buck by surprise. He'd noticed a big cloud ahead, almost like that of a thunderstorm. But the sky otherwise showed no sign of such a storm. It turned out to be the dust rising as the big shaggies moved from one place to another.

It was hard to imagine how many there were in this one herd. There were definitely hundreds, or perhaps thousands. However many there were, Buck was amazed. He'd heard the stories of their vast numbers, the size of the black, burly animals, and how easy they were to kill. Already there was talk of killing off the herds to the point that some folks were siding with the Indians in their belief that restrictions should be imposed to prevent their massacre. It was hard to imagine, however, as Buck gazed at the vast number of creatures, that some day they could be all gone.

Buck decided that he would not attempt to shoot a buffalo. He had plenty of food for the time being, and it was surely no sport to ride up to a slow, clumsy animal and shoot him down. Somehow this just didn't seem right to him at the time. And besides, Blaze seemed mighty reluctant to chase after them. The smell, the number of the animals, the dust they created, and who knows what else, caused Blaze to balk.

"OK Blaze," Buck said. "We'll wait on this for the time being. Maybe another day."

With that, Buck reined Blaze a little more west of the herd and set him into a gentle slow lope. It wasn't long before he spotted something he more easily recognized on the horizon...cattle.

As he approached the herd of cattle Buck noticed riders flanking them on all sides. It was evident to him that the cowboys were moving them in a general northwestward direction, but he couldn't tell much more than that. He decided to approach the herd and strike up a conversation with one of the men. After all, it had been quite sometime since he'd talked to anyone.

Buck headed Blaze to the rider nearest him. He was obviously riding drag on the herd, usually the worst, and certainly the dirtiest job on any drive. As Buck approached him, the cowboy noticed him coming and he stopped, turned his mount toward him, and prepared for the meeting.

"Howdy," Buck offered as he approached the cowboy. "I'm Buck Ward, and I'm headed for the New Mexico Territory. Saw you boys on the trail and thought I'd ride over and talk a while."

"That's mighty fine with me, mister," came the answer. "I don't get to talk to many strangers, or anybody else for that matter."

The response came from a mere boy. He couldn't have been more than fourteen or fifteen years old. He appeared to be tall for his age, but he was really skinny, with freckles covering his face, at least what Buck could see of it. The boy's hat was pulled down low around his ears, and his face was so dirty that it was hard to see through the dirt. He rode a nice bay gelding, with black legs, mane and tail. His saddle was well worn, but was made well, telling Buck that whoever bought it for the boy knew quality when he saw it.

"Where you headed?" Buck asked.

"We're movin' this bunch of longhorns over to the north pasture, about ten or twelve miles up yonder," the youth responded with his finger pointed to the north. "Pa's afeared that the grass here, what little there is of it, will never make it, come summer, if the whole herd stays put."

"Oh, your pa is the boss of this outfit?" Buck responded.

"Sure is, mister. My pa owns practically all of this part of the country. Calls it the Lucky 4, 'ceptin' I ain't so sure why. I ain't ever shared in none of that luck."

"Where would I find your pa?"

"He's the one over yonder," the boy said as he took his hat off and pointed in the direction of the rider on the west side of the herd.

"Much obliged, son," Buck responded as he nudged Blaze in the flanks. "Hope to see you again."

"By the way, my name's Cody," the boy yelled as Buck made his way toward the owner of the Lucky 4.

Buck had no idea why the notion came over him to see if he could catch on with this outfit for a while. After all, it would only delay his arrival in the New Mexico Territory, and he never had any definite plans to stay anywhere along the way for any significant amount of time. But there was something that caused him to want to try his hand here. And this might be as good a place as any.

The boy's pa had seen him talking to Cody and watched Buck closely as he drew closer and closer. Buck could imagine how suspicious he might be, so he tried to be as friendly as possible as he approached.

"Sir, are you Cody's pa?" Buck asked upon riding into hearing distance.

"That's right, I'm Lance Thorn, owner of the Lucky 4. And who might you be, stranger?"

"Name's Buck Ward, from down south of Ft. Worth. I'm headed for the New Mexico Territory, but thought you might could use a rider for a while. I'm plumb short on supplies, and I could use a dollar or two to keep goin' on this trek."

"Well, I understand your predicament, but I like to get to know folks a little better 'fore I offer them a job. Tell you what though, you follow us on in to camp, we'll talk around supper tonight, and if'n I get the right hunch about you, we'll talk about a job."

"Sounds fair enough," Buck responded. "Any particular place you want me to get?"

"Naw," Mr. Thorn answered. "Just fit in wherever you please."

Buck decided to ride up further toward the front of the herd. He'd noticed a place where the herd seemed to be a little loose. He felt that he could shore up this area as they drove on to the north pasture, as Cody put it.

As Buck began working the cattle he got a renewed sense of the value cowboys held in these extreme cattle raising situations. Cows were dumb animals, about as dumb as any you'll ever cross. They don't know much about anything except eating and caring for their young. Everything else has to be directed by these cowpunchers. And Buck was good at it because he'd had so much experience on horseback, and his pony was one of the best. With just a nudge of the knee Blaze would move quickly to cut off the path of an ornery steer. And Buck's rope proved to be useful also. Twice he roped strays that had got away from the herd and dragged them back, utilizing the strength of Blaze in the process.

After two or three hours of riding herd the terrain began to slowly change. Small mounds or buttes appeared ever so often. Buck had never seen anything like this before. He got excited as he saw these, realizing that a bigger thrill would eventually come when he got a glimpse of the Rockies for the first time!

It wasn't long before the cowboys at the front of the herd began slowing the pace and Buck could tell that they were nearing their destination. He noticed that the area they were approaching had more grass than where they'd come from, and he could see a creek ahead, with a few willow trees in clear sight. In this part of the country, water was a precious commodity, and he could easily see why this little valley would be a good place to leave the herd for the time being.

Mr. Thorn soon led a small group of the cowboys he'd called on back to the point where Buck was. As he approached he had a big smile on his face.

"Ward, you fit in mighty fine durin' your time with us today. I'll confess that I ain't seen a horse in a while better suited to trail herding than that chestnut of yours."

"Thanks, Mr. Thorn," Buck responded. "I'm right proud of him. Guess he's about the only thing I own that I wouldn't part with for the right price."

"I hate to hear that," Thorn replied. "I was about to make you an offer for him. Well, anyway, we can talk horseflesh later. We're headed over to the headquarters now. Fall in with the rest of us and we'll be sittin' before a plate of beans and potatoes before you know it."

Buck followed as he was told. He could sense that the rest of the hands in the group were still a little suspicious of him. They eyed him pretty good, but several spoke briefly as they rode away, mostly just saying hello and some tipping their hats.

There were five riders with the group other than Mr. Thorn and Cody. All rode mustang-type steeds, none of which would be able to stay with Blaze in a good race. In fact, as they rode, Buck had to hold Blaze back to a slow lope while most of the others labored to stay at that pace without running all out.

One of the riders had introduced himself as Jake. He seemed to be the leader of the group. He was tall and lanky, with dark black hair and a slight scar on his right cheek. He packed a six-shooter on his hip, and a Remington carbine was slung from the saddle on his palomino pony. Something about this rider caused Buck to be cautious about him. Although he couldn't put a finger on why he felt this way, Buck's past experience with men of all types told him to watch Jake closely.

The other men didn't give their names immediately, but Buck could tell they knew what they were doing when it came to handling cattle. One appeared to be more than sixty years old, with a gray beard covering his face. Another was a little younger, but his face revealed the long hours of sun baked work on the range. A third rider was called Rusty, obviously because of his red hair and freckled face that gave the appearance of orange. The final rider was a young man, perhaps in his early twenties, and the handsomest of the group. Even after riding all day long he looked fresh when compared to the others. Buck imagined that he was definitely the ladies' man of the group.

Buck talked with Cody as they rode along toward the headquarters. Cody was full of questions, and it was evident that he'd not talked to a stranger for a while. He wanted to know about anything and everything that had happened to Buck along the way.

"Tell me about them dance halls in Ft. Worth," he said. "I hear tell there's some wild nights go on there."

"Fact is, I can't say that I know about that Cody," Buck answered. "I was only there one night, and I got run out of one of them there places before it got plumb dark!"

"How'd that happen?" Cody asked.

"Well, it's a long story, one I better tell you later. Now, tell me something, what's the setup at the headquarters, and who'll be there when we get there?"

"Aw, there ain't much there. Our house is situated in the middle of it all. There's a bunkhouse for the boys, two barns and a corral or two. Ain't nobody there 'cept for Mama and Lucy."

"Who's Lucy?" Buck asked.

"She's my sister. Gives me more trouble than you could shake a stick at. I'll be glad when and if she ever gets married off."

"Sounds like a normal family relationship," Buck said with a grin. "How old is this terrible sister of yours?

"She's eighteen, but acts like she's my mother," he replied. "I'll teach her to boss me one of these days."

About that time Buck caught a glimpse of the buildings from a far distance. It was just about dusk, and he could faintly make out the outline of the headquarters. It was different than he had pictured in his mind from Cody's description. A bit bigger than he thought, and the location was nicer, with big trees surrounding the area, something he'd not seen for quite a while now.

The men rode in and right up to one of the barns.

"All right men," Mr. Thorn ordered, "unsaddle, get a little of that dust off you, and I'll see you at mess in a few minutes. Ward, for the time being, you go with Cody there. He'll show you around."

"Yes, sir," Buck responded, "and thanks for your kindness."

Buck left Blaze in front of the main house and followed Cody in. The house was big, perhaps bigger than any he'd ever been in before. It was made of native rock, reddish in color, and was two stories tall. A wide porch went all the way around it, and there were several chairs scattered here and there.

The two of them walked in the front door and into a large room where a huge stone fireplace was burning. The room looked cozy and gave Buck an immediate warm feeling. He saw stairs leading to the upper story, and doors going from this main room that lead to others, with one more than likely being the kitchen.

"Hello, Cody. Who's your friend?" The remark came from one of the doorways and quickly caused Buck to turn to notice who it was.

"This here's Buck . . . I ain't rightly rememberin' his last name, Ma," Cody said with more than a little embarrassment showing on his face.

"Name's Buck Ward, ma'am," Buck replied. "I've asked your husband for a job and he's tryin' to make up his mind if'n I'm worthy."

"Well, make yourself at home, Mr. Ward. Supper will be served shortly," she said as she left the room with a slight smile on her face.

Mrs. Thorn was not a handsome woman. Buck could easily tell that the rough ranch life, the hot sun, and the physically demanding jobs these pioneer women had to perform had made her age more than her years. Nevertheless, she was dressed nicely, and he sensed a pride about her that was becoming.

"Let's go up to my room, Buck," Cody said.

"Sure," Buck responded.

They headed up the big oak staircase, obviously rough-hewn by hand. Cody almost ran up, but Buck took it a bit more slowly, trying to notice whatever he could as he went up.

At the top of the stairs a runway went both directions, with two rooms on each end. Cody headed to the left, so Buck followed. As they went by the first room Cody announced, "That's Lucy's room. I stay clear of there!"

Buck only laughed as he followed Cody to his room. It was large, almost as large as the whole house that Buck grew up in. It was also messy, with clothes, boots, and other things lying all around.

Over in one corner was a dresser with a pan filled with water and Cody allowed Buck to wash up first, which he gladly did. Cody splashed as little water on himself as possible and announced that he was hungry, so Buck followed him back downstairs to wait on supper.

Only a few minutes passed until Mrs. Thorn rang a dinner bell hanging on one of the side porches. It didn't take the men long to get there and soon the Thorn family, Buck and all the hired hands were seated at a long table in one of the rooms leading off of the big room he'd first entered.

The food was abundant, with fried chicken being the main course and whole potatoes and red beans on the side. Buck hadn't realized how hungry he was until he'd finished more than his share of the vittles.

Lucy Thorn was seated directly across from Buck, near the far end of the long table. She had long, wavy hair, almost golden in color. Her face was filled with innocence, unlike so many of the women Buck had seen during his stay in Ft. Worth. She was attractive, but not in a way that would stop men in their tracks. However, her smile seemed to bring a warmth to Buck when he first noticed it, and she blushed as she caught his staring while others had their eyes on Mr. Thorn, who was carrying on most of the conversation at the table.

"Dad gummit," Mr. Thorn said. "We plum forgot to say grace. Let's bow now, before the good Lord decides to remind us in some other way. Dear Lord, we thank you for all that you've blessed us with, and especially for this food that sits before us. We ask that you look over all of us, our belongings, and those that need you in special ways. We give you the honor for all good things, and take our share of the responsibility for things that aren't so good. It's in your name I pray. Amen."

Buck seemed to be almost immediately drawn closer to the Thorn family following that prayer. He really couldn't explain it. But the fact that Mr. Thorn relied on the Lord, and proved it by praying aloud, in front of all of his men, made him comfortable with this family. He decided then and there that he was going to repay them for this feeling by working hard for them. That is, he'd do so if Mr. Thorn took a notion to hire him.

"Buck, now tell us something about yourself," Mrs. Thorn said.

Everyone around the table stopped their talking when they heard this question, especially the cowboys. They wanted to size him up fast. Cowboys were usually this way. They made quick decisions, right or wrong, and these hired hands might very well decide if they liked Buck based on this one conversation. And Buck knew it.

"Well," Buck began. "There's really not that much to tell. I hail from Corsicana, down southeast of Ft. Worth. I grew up as an orphan, and spent most of my time alone. This made me grow up a little sooner than most kids, but I ain't complainin' none. I like takin' care of myself. Anyway, I always took to horses, ropin' and the like. Folks that have seen me ride and rope say I'm a natural, but I don't take those words to heart. I just try to work hard, treat people right, and figger that everythin' will come out right in the end."

"Sounds good to me," Mr. Thorn responded. "Something about you, Ward, that I think will make you fit right in here at the Lucky 4. If'n you want, you can move into the bunkhouse tonight, and be ready to go to work bright and early tomorrow morning."

"Thanks, Mr. Thorn," Buck said. "You won't regret this decision."

The rest of the men remained silent during this discussion. Buck tried to measure the effect of his hiring on the men, and he could tell that most had no opinion, but the leader of the cowboys, the one called Jake, responded differently. Buck could see in his eyes an almost instant twinge of jealousy. And he'd seen it enough before to know that that look could cause him trouble later on. He'd not be forgetting to watch his backside when the situation called for it.

As soon as supper was over, Buck excused himself from the table and headed outside. He found Blaze, untied, in the same spot he left him. After all these years together, this fact continued to amaze him.

He quickly unsaddled Blaze after noticing that there would be room for him in the nearby corral. He carried the saddle over his shoulder while leading the horse to the gate. The corral was a sturdy one, made of cedar posts, and the gate swung open easily as Buck slapped Blaze on the rear to make him go in. The horse obliged and headed at a lope to the water and hay on the far side.

"Don't make yourself sick," Buck ordered as he turned and hung the saddle over the fence.

Ordinarily Buck would have taken his saddle inside, but in this dry, arid climate there would be no problem with leaving it out. He then gathered his bedroll, took the rifle from the scabbard, and grabbed his saddlebags to tote to the bunkhouse.

The bunkhouse was probably a hundred yards away from the corral. It was a big building, but built in a simple, yet sturdy way. It was long and rectangular in shape, and was constructed out of cedar planks. There was a long porch extending the length of the front of the building. On it Buck saw two or three men lounging around, obviously trying to relax after a hard day's work.

"Look's like we'll be workin' together, Ward," offered one of the men as Buck approached. "Name's Alston, Jesse Alston."

"Call me Buck," he said, offering his hand for a shake.

Alston's shake was that of a real man. He was strong, and Buck could tell from the coarseness of his skin that this man knew how to work. He appeared to be close to forty years old. His face was typical of a cowboy of those days, deeply tanned and wrinkled from too much time spent in the sun. He had long, wavy brown hair protruding from the dirtiest, most wrinkled looking hat you'd ever see. It was obvious that this man didn't think much about how he looked.

"You can bunk right next to me if you want," he said. "Go in the door, count four beds to your right, and that's mine. The next one is a spare."

"Much obliged," Buck responded. "I'll take you up on that."

When Buck walked in he immediately noticed the smell of sweaty cowboys. Cowboys weren't noted for their cleanliness, with most not taking a bath for weeks at a time. Since most of them owned only one or two shirts and a pair of pants, they were dirty more than they were clean. And when you found several of them cooped up in a confined area together, you could usually notice it with your smeller.

The room itself was well kept. Most of the bunks had been made up that morning, and there was very little clutter around on the floor. A couple of the cowboys were already lying in their beds, even though it was early yet.

On the far end of the room there was a giant fireplace, covering almost the entire wall. It was made of stone, stone that Buck figured to have been gathered from close by. There were ledges on the fireplace where men could sit, tell stories, sing, or anything else they took a liking to. Buck imagined that if he stayed around until winter he'd enjoy that fireplace. However, he quickly thought to himself that it wasn't likely that he'd be here that long.

It wasn't long until most of the men had made their way into the bunkhouse. Buck visited with two or three of them briefly, but confined most of his talk with Jesse Alston. He liked this cowboy, and the more they talked the more he realized that they shared much in common, other than age.

There was a lamp on a table close to Buck's bunk so he thought he'd have time to drop a line to his old friend Lyle. He grabbed the saddlebags from under his bed, found lead and paper, and wrote the following.

Dear Lyle,

Thot I'd tell you where I was now, not that it'd make much diffrence to anybody where I am. I've just hired on at a ranch here in the panhandle. It's called the Lucky 4 and owned by a reel square man named Thorn. He has a nice famly and several riders.

Tomorrow will be my first day to work here. I'm lookin forward to it. Guess cause I've been doin nothin but ridin by myself for so long now.

Two things I can't get off my mind. Kelly and them boots. Lyle, I know you can't do much about Kelly, but could you buy them boots I wanted and hold em until I find a way to get em to me? I'd be much obliged.

Your frinship meens a heap to me, Lyle. You'll be hearin more from me on down the road.

Your Frind,

Buck Ward

Buck folded the letter neatly, addressed it to Lyle in Ft. Worth, and put it back into his saddlebags so that he could get it mailed as soon as possible.

Most of the men had settled in for the night by now. Buck had been almost oblivious to what went on around him while he was thinking and writing. He found that he was often like this when Kelly was on his mind. He didn't think he'd ever really get over her, but he knew that he'd better start trying if he was going to have a decent life from here on.

⌘

Chapter Ten

Buck awoke the next morning to the ringing of the dinner bell. From the darkness of the sky he knew that it was before sunup. That didn't really surprise him none, but no one had said what time they'd get a start this morning.

He quickly got dressed, and even roused one or two of the other riders from their stubbornness to get up. Jesse was one of those, and he could tell very quickly that he wasn't the kind of man you would want to bother when he was first getting up in the morning.

The men were called to a big breakfast, consisting of biscuits and sausage gravy, with plenty of coffee for washing it down.

After the men had eaten, Mr. Thorn hollered for all to gather around in front of the porch, with horses saddled and ready for work. Buck complied with this directive and soon everyone was waiting for orders.

"Listen now, men," Mr. Thorn started. "Today's gonna be a big day on this here spread. We got lots of brandin' to do, strays to round up, and the big herd needs to be moved to another location."

After this introduction, Mr. Thorn proceeded to give each man orders for what they were to do that day. Thorn was firm but fair. However, this sense of fairness didn't keep him from making these riders work for their pay, and Buck had heard more than one cowboy complain in the bunkhouse last night about this.

"Jake, I want you and Ward here to ride to the west boundary, gathering strays as you go, and bring back what you find. I expect it may take you all day to do this, so go there to the kitchen and grab some of them biscuits to take to get you through the day. There might be a little jerky you could take along also."

Buck could immediately sense that Jake didn't like these orders. He responded to Mr. Thorn by saying, "But

Mr. Thorn, I rode that route just the other day. Don't you think..."

Before he could get anything else out Mr. Thorn interrupted. "Jake, you heard my orders. Now, let's get to it."

Buck went over to the house and got the vittles as instructed. Jake didn't comply with this directive, so Buck got a little extra to share. However, he sensed that this rider was going to be trouble, and he didn't feel that the offer of a biscuit or two was going to make a difference in that.

The two men rode out from the headquarters just as the sun was rising behind them. It was going to be a nice day, and would probably be hot before the day was up. Buck trailed behind Jake for a while, but had some trouble staying there. Blaze was a good deal taller than Jake's mount, and his lope caused him to close in on the shorter horse in short order. Finally, after maybe thirty minutes of riding, Buck pulled up alongside of Jake.

"Got any plan for how to carry out these orders?" Buck questioned.

"Stay out of my face, Ward," came the response.

"Why don't you tell me what's eatin' at you, Jake," Buck countered. "It's plain to see that you got a burr in your saddle about somethin'. Let's get it out in the open now."

"I'm warnin' you right now," Jake hollered. "Don't get me riled."

Buck hated to start the day with a fight but he figured that one would come sooner or later. So he responded by remarking, "Looks to me like you get your way a lot around here. Well, I'm one cowpoke who won't take nothin' from you, and you'd better get that in your head right now. As a matter of fact, I'd just as soon settle this right here and now."

With that said Buck pulled up on the reins and brought Blaze to a stop. Jake did the same with his mount and both riders quickly dismounted and faced each other.

"How do you want your medicine?" Jake asked.

"You choose," came Buck's reply. "I'm game for whatever."

Jake noticed the cool response that Buck gave. This was the same coolness that had riled men before, and was the mannerism that seemed to give Buck the edge when these issues had arisen with men before.

"I choose six-shooters," Jake said. "Right here and now."

Buck was a bit shocked to think that this man would risk his life because of a disagreement like they'd had. It pointed to a bigger problem this man had, and Buck didn't know what that bigger problem was. He did know, however, that he'd never been matched before in gunplay, and he didn't think Jake would be the first.

"All right Jake," Buck responded. "But let me get my gun out first. I got it in my saddle bag right now."

Buck walked back to his pony and pulled the gun from the bag. He promptly rolled the cylinder, making sure it was fully loaded, and stuffed it in its customary position in his front belt.

"Man, you don't even have a gun belt," Jake said. "I'm gonna feel guilty boring you."

Buck knew at that point that Jake was bad news. Any man that would consider killing a perfect stranger over nothing had bigger problems to consider. He decided then and there that he would try to avoid killing the man, but he also knew that it would take some doing to accomplish that.

Buck stepped about fifteen paces off between he and Jake and then turned toward him. Jake carried a .45 on his right hip, in a black holster with silver trimmings.

"I'm gonna give you some advice, Jake. I've killed enough men to know that you're not gonna be the one to stop me. And the only reason we're standin' here in this red dirt and facin' each other is that you're bad, and I know it. But you'd better make up your mind right now if you're ready to meet your Maker!"

With that Buck drew his pistol and fired three shots in rapid succession at Jake's feet. He aimed close enough that

Jake jumped in response each time. When the commotion stopped, Jake was looking down the barrel of Buck's gun and had not even had time to think of drawing his own.

Jake didn't know how to respond. He knew in his mind that he was no match for this stranger from Corsicana, but his pride didn't allow him to respond that way.

"You tricked me," he said.

With that Buck fired two more shots close by.

"No, no trick to it. I just saved your life by showin' you who could handle a gun better. You and me both know the answer to that one. Now, this here matter is over. I got work to do, with or without you."

Buck coolly walked back to his mount, all the while keeping his eye on the beaten cowboy. And with one bullet left in the cylinder of his pistol, Buck knew he could stop Jake in his tracks if his nerve overtook his senses.

As Buck rode away he knew that he'd have to keep a close eye on this man as long as he worked at the Lucky 4. It wasn't easy for any man to be embarrassed the way Buck had embarrassed Jake, and Buck knew that he'd try to get even sooner or later.

Buck continued his ride to the west alone. He never saw any other sign of Jake for the rest of the day, but he did manage to round up several head of cattle. Most of them were located in draws or gullies that were out of sight from a distance.

He headed back toward the ranch about mid-afternoon, realizing that it would take him until dark to wrangle the stubborn cattle that far. About a mile or so from the ranch he noticed a lone rider approaching him from the north. He recognized the rider to be Jake and he figured out that Jake didn't want anyone to know about the altercation, so he decided to ride in with Buck as if nothing had happened. When the two men drew within speaking distance, neither one of them said a word to each other.

After supper that night Buck returned to his bunk and spent the rest of the evening thinking and reading. He'd had an eventful day, but no one but Jake and Buck knew it. He spent some time thinking about Kelly, but he was successful in not dwelling on her. Finally, he read a few chapters from the Bible, the book that seemed to be calling him from deep within.

These calls began to haunt Buck's thoughts. He didn't know what to make of them. Aw, he'd heard preachers say before that they were called of God, but he figured that these were just figments of their imaginations. But how could he explain what he was feeling? He considered himself to be a normal, red-blooded cowboy, yet here he was in the middle of the Great Plains and he was being drawn to read from a book that was difficult at best to understand.

He longed for answers to these questions, and reconciled in his mind that he might only find these answers in the Bible itself. Therefore, night after night, Buck read. And it wasn't long before he began to have a clearer understanding of what the words in this ancient book meant.

After only a couple of weeks on the ranch Buck had already gained the reputation as the hardest worker employed by Mr. Thorn. In addition, he was well liked by most of the men, and the Thorn family all seemed to make him their favorite. This applied to Lucy Thorn as well.

One day a few weeks later, Buck was out riding when he noticed Lucy approaching him on her solid black mare. He reined in Blaze and sat there almost motionless as she closed the final distance between her and him. She was a good rider, a fact that Buck had paid attention to before. He also noticed her long, flowing locks of blond hair blowing in the wind as she drew to a stop a short distance from where he waited.

"Howdy, Lucy," Buck offered. "What you doin' way off up here so far from the house?"

"Looking for you," came her reply.

Buck was a bit taken aback by the forwardness of this statement. Most women in those days, certainly those with the character and reputation of Lucy, would have been much more reserved.

"Well, here I am," he replied. "Now what's on your mind?"

"Nothing really," she said. "Just wanted to talk for a moment."

"Well, talk away. Ol' Blaze here needs a rest anyway."

"It's Cody I'm concerned about. Lately he's been different. Kinda short with his responses to Mom and me. I'm afraid he's settlin' in with the wrong crowd. He's been out with Jake lately, and I don't know where they've been going. Anyway, since he's taken such a liking to you, I thought maybe you'd have a talk with him. It'd mean a lot to me if you would."

"Aw, Lucy," Buck began. "You're probably worried for nothin'. That's a good boy if'n I ever saw one."

"But you don't understand, Buck," she argued. "He is different, and I know it's that Jake that accounts for it."

Lucy dismounted at about that time, causing Buck to do the same. She tied her horse to a nearby bush and started walking. Buck followed after dropping his reins to the ground. The two of them lazily walked in the general direction of the nearest tree of any size, a distance of about seventy-five yards. The shade of the straggly Mesquite was inviting, so both Buck and Lucy sat down, with their backs sharing the tree trunk.

"Why do you distrust Jake so much?" Buck asked.

"He's never been any good," came her reply. "He's always fooled Pa in that respect, but not me. In fact, he once made a pass at me. I let him have it good, and he vowed to get even with me one day. I think he's the type of man to do just that."

"You won't have to worry about that as long as I'm around, Lucy."

"Oh, Buck, that's comforting, but I couldn't expect you to stand up to that gunfighter, especially not after what happened between you and him."

Buck's face turned a bit red with anger. "What are you talkin' about, Lucy, when you say somethin' happened between me and him?"

"Everyone's heard about that fight y'all had out on the range that day. He's bragged about it for days now."

"Lucy, I ain't told nobody about what happened that day. Figgered it'd be better for all involved if'n it was kept quiet. But if Jake has told everybody about it already, I guess I might as well set the record straight. And I'll tell you right now, Jake ain't no more of a fast gun than you are, and I would've bored him then and there if'n I knew he was goin' to make up a tale like this one."

With that Buck began to recount the true facts of the encounter. All the while Lucy was looking intently into Buck's eyes and relishing this version of the events. When he concluded the story, she reached up and hugged Buck, catching him totally by surprise.

"Hope nobody seen that from a distance," Buck said. "They might think there was more to it than there really was."

This statement caused Lucy to suddenly change her demeanor. A bit of red showed in her face as she remarked, "Yeah, we sure wouldn't want anyone to get the wrong idea."

Buck was too naive to notice that Lucy's remark had a sarcastic tone. He was also too blind to see that she was falling in love with him.

Lucy and Buck walked back to the horses without saying anything. Buck helped her mount and told her to be careful on her way back. She nodded obligingly, kicked her mount roughly in the flanks, and rode off toward the house.

Lucy's departure caused Buck to begin thinking about how to handle the affair concerning him and Jake. On the one hand, he couldn't bear to think about letting the other cowboys think that a lazy, good-for-nothing drifter like Jake had bested him. His pride was simply too big for that. On the other hand, Buck thought that he might get a better handle on what might be going on with Cody if he didn't raise the issue immediately. Whatever he finally decided on, he knew it would be hard to avoid an immediate confrontation, and when it came, he knew that he might have to kill the man.

Buck finished up his work right before dark and slowly rode back to the ranch. By the time he arrived the other hands had already eaten, so Buck just went to the kitchen and got what he could carry back to his bunk. He lay down on the bunk, snacked on the food he'd brought with him, and began reading from his Bible.

When he was good and full, Jesse Alston came and lay down in his bunk beside Buck. Buck had grown to really like this lonely cowboy. He was a good hand and a good man. Buck could tell from the way he talked.

"Buck," Alston began. "There's been somethin' botherin' me for a while now. I can't say it real loud, so lean over here and listen close."

Buck obliged and moved to the edge of his bed and closed his book for the time being.

"I don't know how to say this, Buck, but the men are really talkin' bad about you. They've been fallin' for the line that Jake has put out on you. I . . . well, Buck . . . he's said. . ."

Buck interrupted him from his stumbling words. "I'll make it easy for you, Jesse. I heard just today that Jake has been spreadin' rumors about a scuffle we had. And I know full well that he's told that he got the best of me. Is that what you wanted to say?"

"You hit the nail on the head, Buck," came his reply. "Tell me it ain't true."

"Do you believe it's true," Buck asked?

"I shore don't," came Jesse's reply. "But the truth of the matter is I can't say for sure. You strike me as the better man in more'n one way, Buck, but you've never said. Fact is, I been defendin' you for two or three weeks, now, and I gotta know if my hunch was right."

"Well, Jesse," Buck responded. "Quit your wonderin'. That no-count cowboy never bested me in anything, and I'm just waitin' for the right moment to confront him with it. I'm afraid it may take gunplay to settle it, though."

"That's a load off my mind, friend," Jesse said. "Can you tell me what did go on out there?"

"Not right now. But I'll fill you in one of these days after this is all settled. Now, there's somethin' I need from you, but we can't afford to talk about it right here and now. Too many ears listenin'. I'll meet you in the mornin' shortly after we ride out, over at Two Buttes. It'll be safe to talk there."

Nothing else was said between the two men that night.

Buck had trouble sleeping during the night. Many thoughts went through his head. He first thought, as usual, about Kelly Stanfield. But he didn't dwell on her like he sometimes did. He thought mainly about Lucy's concern for Cody, and what he was involved in with Jake. And he was going to begin working on that first thing in the morning.

"Come on Grandpa," I said. "Tell us a little more before we have to get some shuteye. You've got us right to the excitin' part."

"And that's exactly where I want you and the boys," he replied. "That way I can use it to get more work out of you."

It seemed that work was the most overused word in the Nichols family. Almost everything revolved around it. But my dreams were always about finding a way not to have to work. I was usually disappointed, though.

I went to bed that night thinking about how old Buck might get the goods on that rascal, Jake, and how he'd probably save Cody from goin' bad. Those thoughts occupied my mind until morning.

It seemed that only a brief period of time had passed when I felt Ma shaking me from a deep sleep. "Get up, boy, before I have to switch you."

Threatening me with a switch nearly always got me to movin'. The fact of the matter was, I'd rather have taken a strappin' from Poppa any time than to get one of Ma's switchin's. Those little pear tree branches she'd cut from time to time would leave marks on my bottom for days afterwards. And when I'd complain to her about it she'd look at me, smile, and say something like, "Travis, the only thing that will help with this situation is for you to do as you're told. When that happens, you won't have to worry about your bottom hurting any more."

Grownups in those days could get away with that kind of attitude. And now that I'm grown, I'm thankful that they did. It caused me to grow up right.

That morning was Saturday and the whole family was looking forward to going to town. We did this about once a month, with the whole family that is, and all of us had our own reasons for being so excited. For my older brothers, they got to take a look at the pretty girls in town. I remember them talking about the young ladies that they wanted to go out with. Mama and Mary Sue would look at frilly dresses in the store windows. Poppa would try to make deals for farm equipment that would help us make a better living. And I would go to Levi's Leather Goods and browse around. Just the thought of the smell of that establishment brings back fond memories.

Once we got back to the house Grandpa offered to continue with Buck's story. Everyone in the family was ready.

⌘

Chapter Eleven

Two Buttes was about four or five miles from the Lucky 4 headquarters. Since Mr. Thorn had instructed Buck to head in that direction to do some branding anyway, no one thought anything unusual about his departure that morning. But Buck himself knew that this day was the beginning of something big for him, he just didn't realize at that time exactly how big.

He caught a glimpse of the two red, rocky formations just as he rode out of Salty Draw, a dry creek bed that covered almost the entire ranch from east to west. Before he got there he saw Jesse and his mount waiting beside a greasewood bush.

"Thought you had forgotten," Jesse offered as Buck and Blaze got within easy speaking distance. "What'd you do, go to town first?"

Buck knew this to be a joke, for the nearest town was too far to have been visited from there by this time of day.

"Fact of the matter is, that's exactly what I did. And I met a purty girl there to boot!"

This drew a laugh from the good-natured cowboy as Buck arrived and dismounted.

"Now tell me what's on your mind, Buck," Jesse stated. "I didn't sleep much last night for thinkin' about what you're up to."

"Well, here it is Jesse. Yesterday Lucy looked me up out on the range and confided in me that she's been mighty worried lately about Cody. Seems that he's been hangin' out a lot with Jake and she's suspicious about their goin's on. Maybe she's just worryin' about nothin', but she's convinced that Jake is up to somethin' bad. And if'n he is, she's afraid that he'll get Cody involved in it too. Anyway, I told her that I'd take a look into it. Jesse, you're the only one on the place that I trust to talk to about it. What's your take on her concerns?"

"I ain't gonna make any bones about it. I think she's right, and I've seen enough with my own two eyes to be plenty suspicious. Let's go over here and sit a spell and I'll spill my beans about it."

The two cowboys slowly walked over to an area that afforded some shade from the morning sun that was already hot despite the time of day. Neither one said a word until they got situated.

"Buck," Jesse began. "Here's what I know. Lately I've seen Jake leave the bunkhouse two or three times real late at night. He tries to be quiet about it, but I got ears like an Injun. He's usually gone for two or three hours, and gets back for just an hour or two of shuteye before mornin'. Now I figger he's up to somethin' no good, but I ain't shore of just exactly what."

"Jesse, the tone in your voice makes me think you got a suspicion about what it might be. Am I right in that?"

"I hate to say, cause it's just gossip at this stage, but knowin' that no-good, two-bit cowpoke the way I do, I'll tell you my hunch. Lately the talk in town is that there's been some raidin' of some of the area homesteads. Ain't been any killin' yet, but several of the smaller spreads have been hit. And it ain't cattle that the thieves have been after. It's money. The Russells over by East Fork plumb had to pack up and go back east."

Buck listened intently to Jesse's concerns. "Why do you suspect that Jake might be involved in some of this?"

"Well, it's like this Buck," Jesse answered. "Jake's been hard to find here lately. When the boss gives him orders, he tries to get them changed by tellin' him that somethin' else needs quicker attention, sorta like it's an emergency. When the boss gives in Jake hightails it off alone, and usually don't get back until late in the day."

"Sounds like you got a hunch all right Jesse, but not a whole lot to go on."

"That's why I hesitated to even say it," Jesse responded. "But fact of the matter is there's a little more to it. On one of those days when he told the boss that he needed to head to the south corner of the place to check on some things, I trailed him. I stayed outta sight so he had no chance to see me. I'll be dadgum if'n that varmit didn't circle after he got away from the ranch and he headed due east on a dead run. I followed him for two or three miles until we got into that flatland over there where I couldn't keep on without bein' spotted. But Buck, you know that the Russells lived right in that direction, within easy ridin' distance if'n a man wanted to get there and back in a day's time. It weren't but two or three days later that I got the word that they'd been robbed."

"That's shore enough to give us somethin' to go on Jesse. But what do you think Cody has to do with all of this?"

"I ain't got no idea," he answered. "My hope is that he ain't gone so far as to get involved in the thievery . . . yet."

"Them's my thoughts too, Jesse. I'd hate to think what it'd do to the Thorns if he was to be involved in somethin' like that. It'd plumb take the heart out of Mr. Thorn, and I know that Lucy would have a hard time gettin' over it. I can tell you one thing. I'm gonna do all I can to find out what I can and save Cody from takin' more steps in the wrong direction."

"I'm with you, Buck," Jesse responded.

The two men walked without talking back to their mounts and rode off in separate directions. However, their thoughts for the rest of the day were on this issue, and each one silently vowed to be a part of the solution to the problem, no matter what that brought them in the way of danger.

That night at the supper table Buck decided to begin tryin' to find out if Cody had really changed the way Lucy had said. Buck normally sat in the same spot at the table, but he chose the place right next to Cody this time. He joked with him a time or two as the meat and beans were being passed around, and he immediately noticed some sort of reluctance on Cody's part to engage in conversation with him. Why, there were times in the recent past that Buck had to nearly force him to leave him alone. The boy had definitely taken a liking to him, but now he seemed different, and all this in just a matter of days.

"Cody," Buck offered. "I was thinkin' about askin' your pa to let you ride with me tomorrow. I need a little help with that bunch of yearlin's up around Moore's Crossin'. What do you say to that?"

"Well . . . Buck . . . I can't say for sure. . . I mean . . ."

Before he could even get it all out, Buck could tell that he didn't want to go with him.

"What you stutterin' so much for?" Buck asked. "I thought you'd like ridin' with me for a change. Guess you've got plumb stuck on ol' Jake for a partner."

When he said this the boy got red in the face, like he didn't want anybody to know that he'd been hanging around with him. Buck had seen this kind of response before, and it usually came when a man was trying to hide something. This young rancher's son was definitely trying to hide something, and Buck was afraid it was something bad.

The next morning bright and early Buck went to Mr. Thorn and asked if he could use Cody as a helper for the next few days. He quickly obliged and Buck went upstairs to his room and rustled him out of bed.

"Get up, you lazy two-bit cowpoke," Buck hollered. "We're a wastin' daylight."

Cody's response was typical of a teenage boy, especially one that wasn't used to having to work so early in the morning.

"Aw, come on," Cody argued. "Let me sleep some more."

Buck didn't give in easily, and before long he had the boy at the breakfast table trying to force him to eat. And Cody didn't like it one bit, either.

"Why do you want me 'specially to go with you Buck? Why don't you take one of the hired hands with you?"

"Don't like their company as much," Buck responded. "And besides that, it's about time you started carryin' your weight around here. You can't live off your pa's good fortunes forever."

"Why not?" he said. "I'm a Thorn, ain't I?"

This tone of voice from the boy only led Buck to believe even more that there was something wrong. Never before had he heard Cody talk so rudely, almost sarcastic in nature.

"Well, if that's the way you want it, forget the whole thing," Buck responded in a serious tone and with a cold look on his face.

As Buck began walking out the door, Cody hollered at him to hold up. "Guess I got nothin' better to do."

As they walked to the barn, Buck could tell that Cody somehow regretted the way he'd talked to him. His attitude changed quickly, to the point that he seemed like his old self. The two saddled their mounts, loaded the necessary gear they needed, and set off toward Moore's Crossing.

The day was still young as they made their way past Two Buttes and on toward this place called Moore's Crossing. Buck had heard that it got its name from an old settler named Adam Moore, who'd come to those parts from up in Indiana. At one time it was a thriving settlement, but the years of wind, no rain, and Indian trouble caused most folks to move on. When Mr. Moore was the only one left, he vowed to leave the area looking like it did when he got there. So, right before he left for greener pastures, he burned the whole town down.

The charred ruins of what was left were now visible to Buck as they topped the highest point for miles around. He could see a few strays here and there, but otherwise Moore's Crossing looked about like it did when Moore left. Off to the east, though, stood one of the gathering corrals that Mr. Thorn had built to make it easier to tend to his scattered herd. Buck and Cody slowly loped their horses toward it as Buck spoke for the first time since they left the ranch.

"Cody, my boy, if you play your cards right you'll own all this yourself someday. You'll be a mighty rich man when that day comes."

Cody responded by saying, "Fact is, Buck, I'm not sure I'm wantin' to be a rancher all my life. It's hard work, and there's no guarantee that you'll make anything out of it."

"Cody, I'm gonna lay it to you straight," Buck began. "I've got a hunch that somethin' has come over you. Me and some of the boys have seen it in you, and that sister of yours has too. Guess your pa and ma are too busy to notice. But I brought you out here for the sole purpose of havin' a heart to heart talk about it. Will you talk about it with me?"

"Ain't got nothin' to talk about," Cody replied. "Can't a man change his mind about things from time to time without everybody callin' his hand on it?"

"Sure, sure," Buck said. "But you got one small problem. You ain't a man, not yet anyhow."

These words raised anger in the boy. "You're one to be spoutin' off about bein' a man. You weren't much of one when Jake called you out that day on the range!"

Buck knew then, for sure, that the boy had been hangin' around with Jake. Jake had filled his mind with untruths about their altercation, and he was now taking Jake's side of the events. Probably after Jake convinced him of what he said had happened, he then began using the effects of the story on the boy to lure him into other things. And those other things were what had Buck worried.

"You shore talk like you got it all figgered out," Buck responded. "And all based on what some no good, lyin' thief says."

The boy's eyes betrayed his desire to conceal his thoughts as Buck used the word thief in describing Jake.

Buck went on by saying, "Now I'm about to say somethin' to you, and I'm only gonna say it once. That good-for-nothin' Jake has been fillin' your head with lies. I got the best of him out on the prairie that day and he came in and, instead of takin' it like a man, he made up some story about beatin' me. The truth is the man is no gunman at all. I've killed several men in my time, and Jake couldn't even be mentioned in the same breath with some of 'em. He's got you fooled, and for a while he had some of the others the same way. Anyway, you now are lookin' to him for somethin' that you're not gettin' from anybody else, and we all think it's for the worse. Jake's gonna take some folks down with him when he goes. I'm gonna be the one that takes him down, and I dang sure hope that you're not one of 'em with him when it happens."

A long silence ensued as the two simply stared out into the open prairie. Buck was all the while thinkin' of what he could further say to prompt Cody into spilling the beans. On the other hand, Cody sat silently wondering if he should or shouldn't say what he knew.

"Listen, Cody, it ain't too late for you to get out of this," Buck continued. "Do the right thing on this. Don't disgrace your family, its good name, and all that your pa has worked for to bring you up right. Let me help you."

Cody, with tears in his eyes now, began to unload the truth about what had been happening. "I swore that I'd never tell, Buck. But the fact is, I've always known in my heart that what you said about Jake was true. He's just got such a good way of makin' you think that somethin' wrong is really somethin' not so bad after all."

"That's a good lesson for you to learn, Cody," Buck responded. "The Bible tells it like this. It says that the ol' Devil will try every trick in the book to make you think that a bad thing is good. Started that way so many years ago when man was first put here, and it ain't changed a lick since. Fact is, a man has to be able to make his own mind up about right and wrong, without any interference from somebody else."

"Guess I've always known that, Buck," Cody inserted. "But it's harder to do than just to talk about it. I know now that talkin' about it is just what I'd better do if'n we're gonna put a stop to the game Jake's got planned."

Cody then began recounting the story of how he'd gotten involved with Jake and his wrongdoings. It all started one day when the two were riding together after a day's work. Jake had asked Cody if he'd ever seen a thousand dollars before. When he answered that he hadn't,

Jake chided him about it. He said that his pa was worth that much and many times more, and that it was a shame that he treated Cody like he was one of the hired hands. He told him how unfair that was, and after talking like that to him for several days in a row, he asked him if he might want to go in with him so he could get his hands on some of that cash. Finally, after much coaxing, Cody had given in.

Cody interrupted his story when one of those big West Texas wind gusts started blowing like a locomotive. A storm was brewing, and the two of them knew instinctively that they'd better head for shelter. The problem was that it was miles to the nearest shelter.

"Looks like a bad one, Cody," Buck said. "I can't believe I brought you out here without noticing the sky. Guess I had my mind on only one thing."

"Same here, Buck. Can't blame it all on you."

"I expect it may be a while before the worst of it hits. Maybe we'd have time to get over to the cliffs by then."

The cliffs, as Buck called them, were probably two or three miles away. This was a place where Indians had lived many years ago. There were sandstone caves in these cliffs, and the Indians had discovered natural shelter there. The protection these Indians had discovered so long ago might prove to provide the same kind of protection for these two stranded cowboys.

"Let's hi-tail it outta here," Buck yelled as he jumped on Blaze. "Ain't got no time to lose."

Buck got worried as he saw the cloud that was quickly approaching from the southwest. He'd seen it like this a time or two in his lifetime, but never had he been out in it so exposed to the elements. The cloud showed a tip or tail protruding downward. No doubt about it, this was a twister in the making, and the two of them had no time to lose.

It was fortunate that Cody rode a fine horse himself. He could almost keep up with the speeding Blaze, and soon they were passing the rocks, greasewood and occasional mesquite bushes in a blur. The horses themselves sensed the seriousness of the affair, and their excitement and wild-eyed response created added concern in Buck's mind. When coupled with the ever-darkening sky, he was as concerned as he'd ever been before. After all, he couldn't shoot or fight his way out of this one. And to make matters worse, he had no idea what they'd do with the horses if they did get to the cliffs in time.

The wind was now blowing harder. The West Texas sand was beginning to kick up something terrible. Their vision was obstructed to the point that they had to just point the horses in the right direction and hope that they'd find their way.

Buck's thoughts somehow, and for some reason, began to wander toward a story he'd read recently in the Good Book. It was the one about the disciples being in the boat with Jesus when the storm approached. The disciples were anxious, as anybody would be. But the Lord challenged them for having so little faith. And He brought them through safely.

Buck began to pray to himself. "Lord, I don't really understand your ways, but I'm in a heap of trouble here. If'n you've a mind to, I'd appreciate some help here. Me and this boy need to get to them cliffs 'fore the storm hits full force. I'd be obliged if you'd help us get there."

The strangest thing happened just about then. For some reason the winds let up and Buck caught a glimpse of the cliffs off to the right. He redirected Blaze toward them and he sensed that they'd have no more trouble getting to shelter. Cody followed as closely as he could, with Buck hollering at the top of his lungs to come on.

"Don't worry none about me. I'm too scared to do anything else," Cody offered in response.

The men raced to a spot where there was a cave just above eye-level, and it looked to be pretty deep into the cliffs. They quickly let the horses go after unsaddling and unbridling them, and climbed the red rock to the potential safety of the cave. Once in, they were delighted to see that it went back a far ways, looking to be at least a hundred feet. They would definitely be safe there until the storm blew over.

"Let's stay here purty close to the opening and watch this thing go by," Buck yelled while still trying to catch the breath he'd lost in all the excitement.

"I don't know, Buck, it might just suck us up with whatever else that gets in its path," Cody responded.

"Aw, Cody, I never knew you was so afraid of a little wind," Buck joked. "Down where I'm from this is just a normal wind gust." Buck laughed a little as he made the last statement, knowing that Cody wasn't buying it at all.

The two stood within ten feet of the opening that might have been six feet tall. Buck had to bend down a good deal to keep from hitting his head, and with Cody beside him they almost filled up the small entrance. What they saw from there was something that neither of them would soon forget.

Twisters were a menace in this part of the country. No one ever knew why so many of them seemed to crop up thereabouts. They'd appear out of nowhere, and would soon be carrying off anything and everything that got in their path. Usually only a hundred yards or so wide, they sometimes stretched for much further. They also could speed through the prairie at amazing speed, or sometimes they sauntered along at a slow pace. No matter what variety, though, it was amazing what they could do.

"Hope the horses can fend for themselves," Buck offered as the two of them squinted through the dust and debris to try to spot them. "I've heard tell that animals seem to be able to resist the wind's effect on them. Lookin' at this now, though, I don't think I believe that one bit."

The worst of the storm was just about to hit. The two could only see dust, rain, and an occasional piece of something that flew by, caught up in the furor of the swirling wind. And the sound, it sounded almost like a freight train as it swept by.

Buck didn't know why he seemed to be in a joking mood at about this time, but he figured that it must have been the Lord's guidance on him to try to make Cody feel a little safer.

"Heard tell one time that after one of these things passed through a ranch that there were some strange things that happened. An old man that was a hired hand there said it turned a four-legged wash pot inside out. Plumb sucked the legs through the iron!"

"What do you take me for?" Cody responded. "I ain't so dumb that I'm gonna fall for that one."

"Guess that is a purty tall story, Cody. Now let's get back away from here where we'll be a little safer, that is if'n we don't run into a bear or somethin' worse at the back of the cave."

The two men rustled back for several steps until it got hard to see well. Ordinarily, the light from the opening would have traveled to the back, but the storm had everything almost pitch black. They just sat there, at first listening to the roar of the wind, but then they got back to the talk about Jake and his activities.

"What was it that Jake got you roped into?" Buck asked.

"Well, fact is it weren't much at first," Cody responded. "The first time I just sat on my horse at the top of Bell's Hill and kept a lookout. Didn't even know what was goin' on and Jake never offered to tell me. He gave me a hundred dollars that day and, like a fool, I never asked where it came from. Only went with him two more times, the last one bein' over toward the Russells. I guess I had it figgered out when I got word that they'd been robbed. Why Buck, I was good friends with the Russell's boy, Wilson, and here I was helpin' rob 'em. I never felt so low as I did that night, and I gave all the money back to Jake that he'd given me. He took it all right, but vowed to turn me in if'n I squealed and he got arrested. I never been in such a fix, and I guess it's why I been actin' so strange lately. Buck, do you think I'm too far in now to get out?"

"Naw, not to my way of thinkin'," Buck responded. "In fact, I've got a hunch that you might be just the one to help me catch Jake red handed. Are you game?"

"Sure, Buck, provided you let me tell my pa what I've been involved in. I gotta get it off my chest."

"You're a good boy, Cody," Buck stated. "You'll make quite a man someday."

Buck then began sharing a plan that he'd devised right there in the cave. He wanted to set Jake up, and he'd use Cody to do it. Cody could approach Jake and say that he'd reconsidered his gettin' out. Then, he would suggest an easy target for them to hit, and Buck would be there waitin'.

"We'll tell your pa the whole story, Cody." "I'll convince him you mean to set things right."

The two had been so involved in their talk that they'd hardly noticed that the storm had blown by. They walked the several paces to the opening of the cave and peered out. Since there was little in the immediate area standing in the first place, there was not a lot of noticeable damage to view. But both of them knew that they were lucky, and that they'd just sat out one of the most terrible acts of God known to man. They both, in their own ways, silently thanked their maker that they were still standing.

Buck was the first to see his horse, standing near a small patch of green grass maybe two hundred yards away. He whistled once, and Blaze came to him on the run.

"There's no tellin' where mine is," Cody said. "And if'n I could find him he'd be hard to catch out here on the open range. Takes a bucket of oats and a lot of work to reel him in, even in the best of conditions."

"Well," Buck said. "We'll saddle up ol' Blaze and ride double till we locate him. Come on, let's get started."

Buck threw the now well-soaked blanket over Blaze's back and began to saddle him up. You could tell Blaze didn't like the wet blanket one bit, but he didn't put up much of a fight. And when both Buck and Cody mounted, he seemed to sense the fact that the two were in a jam, and he offered no more resistance.

As the two cowboys made a circle in the general area, they were amazed at the effects of the tornado. Where there were trees, they were uprooted, many of which seemed to have vanished, leaving holes in the ground where roots once were buried. The usually present tumbleweeds were gone, evidently vacuumed up by the twister's suction. In fact, the prairie looked as though someone had taken a huge broom and swept it clean.

Finally, after about thirty minutes of looking, the two riders spotted Cody's horse, munching on some prairie grass near a dry creek bed. The horse was acting as if nothing had really happened, but as the riders approached he took to his usual escape pattern.

"You'll never catch him without some oats," Cody boldly stated.

"You just watch me," Buck responded. "Now get off ol' Blaze, and I'll teach you a thing or two."

Cody dismounted with a jump to the ground. Buck pulled his lariat rope from its resting place and quickly uncoiled it so that he was ready to throw it when the opportunity arose. He then spurred Blaze in the flanks and voiced some instructions as if the horse could understand.

"Go catch him, Blaze, and let's make a quick go of it."

Blaze immediately responded by heading toward Cody's loose mount. In only about two jumps it appeared that he was at full speed. Buck rode him like he was somehow attached, and in just a moment Cody's black gelding sensed what was happening and laid back his ears to make a get-a-way. However, it was too late now. Buck was twirling the lasso above his head and Blaze's speed was too much to elude. A quick toss from Buck's waving right arm caused the noose to go up and over the frightened horse's head and down around his neck. The fight was over.

As most broke horses will do, all of the fight went out of him when the noose tightened. Without incident he followed Buck and Blaze back to where Cody was standing, a bit in awe of what had just happened.

"Man, Buck, I've never see the likes of that. I'll bet it didn't take you thirty seconds to bring him in."

"Takes a lot of practice," Buck responded. "And a good horse like the one I got." Now get back on and we'll lead him back to where your gear is, and we can rustle on back home."

⌘

Chapter Twelve

As the two of them rode back toward the ranch a newfound bond was apparent when they talked. Cody felt better for having finally come clean regarding his involvement with Jake. And Buck felt like he'd done something good in causing Cody to move in that direction.

The good feeling that Buck had, seemed to totally embrace him. He liked doing good for others, yet his reputation as a gunman somehow always overshadowed that. His struggle with good and evil was not unlike that of most folks. He just seemed to have a stronger influence on those with whom he became involved. His thoughts were more and more on the subject of destiny, his role in life, who he was, and who God was as revealed in his reading of the Bible.

"Cody, when are we gonna talk with your pa about this matter?"

"Soon as we get home," Cody responded. "I don't want to put it off any longer."

"I'm proud of you, Cody," Buck responded. "But let's think about this for a minute. It might be better to visit with your pa when nobody else is around. You never know who might be within earshot. What about waitin' 'til mornin' after everybody else has rode out?"

"I guess that's OK, Buck. But I'll have a hard time sleepin' tonight for sure."

"Me, too, Cody. Me, too."

Buck's voice trailed off at the end as they approached the ranch. The two were tired, and agreed to say nothing else to each other until morning, when Mr. Thorn issued orders for the day. Buck was to privately ask Mr. Thorn to assign him and Cody together to stay at the ranch to do some doctoring of some new calves. It was then that they planned to talk with him about Jake and Cody's involvement.

Supper went by without incident. Buck had a brief opportunity to talk with Mr. Thorn privately, and the two told the others of their plight with the tornado. Seems it actually went by the ranch headquarters almost unnoticed because it must've been eight to ten miles from the cliffs to the ranch. "Only saw a black cloud from here," Mrs. Thorn remarked. "I'd have been worried to death if I'd known you two were in such danger."

Buck then retired to the bunkhouse to rest and read from the Good Book prior to going to sleep. His eyes opened wide when he noticed an unopened letter lying on his bed. Addressed to MR. BUCK WARD at the Lucky 4 Ranch, right up in one corner it read BLACKSMITH LYLE.

Buck couldn't think of anyone he'd rather hear from than Lyle, unless it was perhaps . . . yes . . . there was no use in trying to ignore it . . . Kelly Stanfield. But Buck had reconciled the fact in his mind that he'd never see her again. After all, he was headed for the high country and she was back home in Corsicana.

Buck literally tore open the brown envelope that contained his letter and he was excited to see, not just a short note, but a rather long letter.

Dear Buck,

Hope this finds you in good health. Been aiming to write you ever since I got that last note from you. Weren't sure how to get it to you but decided that the Lucky 4 might be well known enough to get this through. Son, next time you send a letter, put a return address on it so I can keep track of you!

First thing is, I got them boots for you. Hope they're the right size. Man, they sure are purty! Never seen a nicer pair, and I talked Old Man Marshall into taking a couple of dollars off the price to boot. I'll try to get them to you as soon as I know for sure exactly where you are and whether the delivery will be safe.

Got some more news for you. That girl you used to be hung up on, Kelly Stanfield showed up at the stables yesterday. I knowed you swore off her a long time ago, but thought you'd want to know. Seems she heard that you followed her to Ft. Worth and she came back a lookin' for you. She found out that you stayed here and came askin' all sorts of questions. I know it's too late, but Buck, that girl is purtier than a west Texas sunset, and I could see in her eyes that she loved you. I told her you had headed west, for the Rockies, and that was about all I knowed. She looked like her world was gonna cave in when I told her that. She left with tears in her eyes, headed back for Corsicana, I guess.

Ft. Worth is still gettin' bigger and wilder by the day. New mercantiles springin' up left and right, and we've even got a new saloon opening right down the street. If you ever get back to this part of the country, you won't recognize the place.

Buck, I hope your leanin' toward trouble has changed there in the panhandle. I guess you know I took a real likin' to you and I want the best for you. Try walkin' away from trouble. You'd be surprised at how it helps you to live longer!

Guess I better go for now. Drop me a line when you can.

Best Wishes,

Lyle

Buck felt a little light-headed when he read the part about Kelly. He re-read it several times, with his mind all the while wandering back and forth from one thought to another. There was no doubting it. He still loved her, and all his attempts to get her out of his mind were without success. How could he rid himself of thoughts of her? Was what Lyle said really true? Did she love him, too? Were her tears those of regret or simply disgust? These and other questions and thoughts entered, left, and then re-entered his mind through the course of the evening. So much so that he hadn't noticed his friend, Jesse Alston, trying to get his attention.

"Buck, Buck, Buck!" Jesse hollered.

"Wha . . . What?" Buck answered as if he were in a far away world.

"Man, what do ya have on your mind tonight? You've been sittin' there starin' at that letter for more'n an hour now."

"Aw, nothin'. Just a letter from an old friend of mine. He's a blacksmith in Ft. Worth."

Jesse responded by saying, "Don't try to fool me, Pard. The way your eyes have been glazed over, you been thinkin' about a girl."

"Well, I won't lie to you. Ole Lyle did mention a girl I once knew. But them times are way behind me now. I've got better things to do that to be hung up on a two-timin' girl."

Buck said these words but he didn't really mean them. He longed for the love of a woman. Even in his resistance to Lucy Thorn's interests he had realized that the natural attraction of a man for a woman was something that he missed. He remembered the warm embraces, the scent of perfume, the brush of soft hair, and the gentle touches. All of which had eluded him since his trek west. Resistance to the affections of a woman would be harder and harder to muster. But he would keep trying, because he felt that any succumbing to Lucy's advances would eventually only lead to heartbreak . . . for her . . . because he knew now, more than ever, that he still loved Kelly Stanfield.

Little sleep came to Buck that night. After tossing and turning for hours, he finally got up well before the rest of the men. He put on his pants and struggled to get his tight boots on, then stepped outside to get some air.

The morning was cool and crisp, the first sign that the summer's heat was fading and that the relief of fall was on the horizon. Nevertheless, his mind quickly moved from thoughts of the coming weather to his plan to put the crooked Jake out of business. He seemed to be obsessed with the desire. It was within his power to save Cody, the good name of the Thorns, and to protect the unsuspecting settlers who Jake was preying on. Nothing could stop him from this.

Finally, after wandering aimlessly and thinking only about the plan, morning broke and the bell signaling breakfast rang out. Buck was the first one to respond, and the smell of sausage, biscuits and gravy, and fresh-brewed coffee aroused his appetite. The fact that he'd been up so long contributed to his hunger, and he gobbled up all he could hold without saying much to the other men.

As usual, Mr. Thorn gave out orders to each of the hands in a gathering right after breakfast. True to his word, he assigned Buck and Cody to stay on at the headquarters and all others were told to disperse to the appointed assignments. The men left in a hurry, leaving only Mr. Thorn, Buck and Cody, other than the womenfolk, in the immediate area.

"Mr. Thorn," Buck began as the three of them walked toward each other. "Like I told you last night, me and Cody have somethin' important to talk to you about. It might take us a while to get it all out. Can we go over to the corrals so we'll be sure this is totally private?"

"My goodness, son," he replied. "Ain't nobody else here except Mama and Lucy. Are you afraid of them hearing this, too?"

"Fact is, sir, we only want you to know what we've got in mind. Could be that your wife and Lucy would be safer if'n they didn't know about this."

Mr. Thorn's face grew tense as Buck made this remark. He immediately sensed the seriousness and walked without comment over to the corral area, a good hundred yards away from the house.

The three gathered in a close circle, with Buck leaning against one of the live oak rail posts and the two Thorns facing him.

Buck began. "Mr. Thorn, first of all, I ask you to hear us out completely before you say anything. You'll want to jump in, I know, but we ask you to let us get it all out first."

"I'll agree," Mr. Thorn reluctantly replied.

Cody started the story.

"Pa," he began. "I'd rather take a lickin' than tell you this. But here goes. I been runnin' with the wrong crowd here lately. Fact is, I now know I was wrong, and I'm willin' to take whatever medicine you want to fork out. Anyway, a few weeks back I started ridin' with Jake and some of his pals at night. At first we just went out and did some drinkin', but then it took a worse turn. I started watchin' out for them. At first, I really didn't know what they was doin'. Then, by the time I figgered it out, I was in way too deep. I guess I knew they was robbin' somebody, but I just couldn't get up enough nerve to stand up to 'em. Then, when I finally got up the nerve, they had the goods on me, too. Told me I'd go down with 'em if I squealed. I didn't know what to do, Pa, 'til Buck here forced me to talk. We spent a whole day together just plannin' out what I should do. Anyway, I'm now ready to set things right."

"That's right, Mr. Thorn," Buck interrupted. "Cody shouldn't be held responsible. After all, he's just a kid, and now we've got a plan to make things right. Will you listen to our plan?"

No response was forthcoming from the red-faced owner of the Lucky 4. Buck could tell that he was trying to hold his temper, so rather than wait any longer he went ahead and outlined the plan.

"Mr. Thorn, that Jake is a no-good son-of-a-gun that needs to be run out of this country. He's got one or two men here at the ranch that is just as bad. I mean to be the man to get rid of 'em all."

"And, Pa," Cody interrupted. "I aim to help him by settin' a trap for him."

About that time a door slammed at the ranch house and Lucy headed to where the men were gathered. They quickly changed the subject as she approached them.

"What's this little meeting about?" Lucy asked. "You're acting like it's a big secret."

Mr. Thorn wasn't much of a liar, but he bluntly responded by saying, "Girl, it ain't none of your business what we're talkin' about. Haven't you got work to do in the house?"

This cold response embarrassed Lucy, especially right there in front of Buck. After all, she wanted to impress the handsome cowboy, to win his love for her, and this was no way of going about it. Rather than argue though, she simply ran back to the house, her blonde curls blowing in the wind.

"Now, what's this about a trap?" Mr. Thorn asked.

"That's what I was about to tell you, Pa, before we was interrupted."

Buck broke in by saying, "Let me tell this part, Cody. After all, it was my idea to drag you into this plan, not yours."

"OK," Cody said.

"Mr. Thorn, my plan is to set him up. I've gotten to know the Cains who moved into the old Crenshaw place last year. They are good people, the kind of folks who would want to help rid this country of hombres like Jake and his pals.

"Sounds fine so far," Mr. Thorn responded. "But how are you gonna pull it off?"

"Here's how, Mr. Thorn," Buck answered. I'm gonna hide out at their place, along with you, if you are willin'. Cody's role is to offer the bait. He'll tell Jake that the Cains have a strongbox full of money they brought here from out east. He'll tell them right where it is in the house and we'll be awaitin' for 'em. Of course, there is no money at the ranch, and we'll get the Cains out of there the night before in case of trouble."

After a moment's pause, Buck concluded by saying, "That's it, Mr. Thorn. The plan's all laid out for your approval."

Mr. Thorn was silent for several more moments. After scratching his head and shaking it in a side-to-side motion, he spoke out.

"I don't know about this. Sounds like a job for the law, but the nearest sheriff is more than a hundred miles away. And I've been told he's not much better than the outfit we're after. By the time we could get him over here there's no tellin' what could happen. On the other hand, if things don't go right with this trap someone could get hurt. . . and I mean hurt bad! I'm just a little uneasy about the whole thing."

"Don't blame you one bit, Mr. Thorn," Buck answered. "I feel the same way. But I can't think of another way that we can get the goods on Jake and his gang of thieves. Now what do ya say? Will you go along with us?"

"I guess I'll have to. Here I've got a boy involved, but at least he's man enough to be willin' to go straight. That don't mean, Cody, I won't hold you responsible for what you've already done. But I guess that issue will hold until all this other is settled. There'll be a day of reckoning, though," he said as he looked straight at his son.

"Pa, I understand, and you won't get no back talk from me, whatever my punishment is," Cody responded.

"Now, boys," Mr. Thorn insisted. "When are you aimin' to pull this off?"

Buck thought a moment, and then spoke up.

"The sooner the better, I'd say. I'll take a day or two to train ole' Cody here in the fine art of lyin', without anyone suspectin' it. Then we'll lay the trap."

"Guess it's time to get to work then, boys," Mr. Thorn barked. "And I mean ranch work, so y'all get after it."

Mr. Thorn walked away, leaving Buck and Cody alone to talk things out.

"Well, that went purty good," Buck said. "Now let's go get to work."

The rest of the day went quickly. The two of them spent most of their time working with the yearlings, but all the while they talked of their plan. Buck emphasized to Cody the need to keep a straight face and to really do a sales job on Jake. They discussed the need to keep their distance from each other, and even planned a disagreement or two between themselves. This was meant to keep anyone from being suspicious and tying the two of them together. And above all, Buck cautioned Cody to not talk to another living soul about the matter. This was dangerous business, and keeping quiet about it might save someone's life.

The next day's activities came and went without incident. Buck spent the evening hours on his bunk reading a newspaper that one of the newer cowboys had brought in and passed around. The biggest news was an account of a fight between some buffalo hunters and Quanah Parker, the Comanche chief. The Indians had attacked the party of hunters at Adobe Walls, not too far from the Lucky 4. Among the hunters was Bat Masterson, who later became notorious for his prowess with a gun. The hunters were able to hold on without being overtaken by the redskins.

As Buck read the account he couldn't help but think of his close encounter with the two Comanches. He knew he was lucky to still be alive. Now he was about to get involved in another dangerous situation. What caused him to be put in these situations? Why couldn't he simply look the other way? Would his life always be like this? With these thoughts whirling in his mind, he fell soundly asleep.

⌘

Chapter Thirteen

The next morning found Buck uncharacteristically nervous. He usually had to rely only on his own prowess. Now he was banking on that of a teenage boy! Much could go wrong, and he found himself thinking about someone else getting hurt rather than himself.

At about midday Buck was off to himself doing some searching for strays. Mr. Thorn liked to use him in this way because Buck and Blaze could cover more ground faster than any other team. As he was working a dry creek bed, he was somewhat startled to see Lucy approaching on her paint gelding.

"Buck, I've got to talk to you," she yelled as she approached and began dismounting.

"Lucy, I can't believe you rode all the way out here by yourself. This is a dangerous country, and a young lady like you shouldn't be here alone. But, never mind, how'd you find me anyway?"

"Pa told me you'd be in this area. He spoke against my coming, but I insisted. You know how he can't say no to me when I insist, my being his little girl and all."

"Yea, Lucy, there'll be lots of men who have that problem before you're too much older. You're a purty girl, and I've heard more'n one man say so."

Buck's remarks were not ordinary for him. As soon as he said them he knew that he shouldn't have. He did not mean to lead her on, but Lucy's eyes sparkled as she heard the words.

"Oh, Buck," she said. "I didn't think you ever paid any attention to a pretty girl."

"I meant no offense, Lucy, " Buck responded. "But now that I've said it, I'm gonna say more."

Lucy prepared herself for something different than what she was to hear.

"Lucy," Buck began. "I aim to set matters straight with us. You shore are the purtiest girl in these parts. If I, or any man for that matter, had any sense, I'd give you all the attention that I could. But the fact of the matter is, I can't, for two reasons. One, I can't tell you. But the other is because I fell in love with one girl already. She took up with another man, but I can't get her out of my head. I'm thinkin' of her all the time . . . to the point that I'm no good to anybody, especially you. I just don't want to hurt you or your family in any way."

Lucy's face turned red as she listened to Buck's stinging words. She was being scorned by the only many she'd ever shown interest in, yet, somehow, she controlled her thoughts enough to not act as hurt as she really was.

"I'll bet I know what that other reason is," Lucy remarked.

"No, you're wrong there, Lucy. Nobody could know that."

"Could it be the plan you and Cody and Pa dreamed up to catch Jake?" she questioned.

Buck's expression turned quickly to anger as Lucy asked the question. "How could you know about that?" Buck responded.

"Cody let it slip out. But please don't be too mad at him. I'll keep it a secret."

Buck pondered his next move in light of this most recent discovery. After all, if Lucy knew, others might also. This was too dangerous of a game to be gambling his life, and the lives of others, if the plan was not bound by secrecy.

"Are you sure none of the other hands, or even your mother, has caught wind of this?" Buck asked. " Cause, if'n you're not, we better drop these plans here and now."

"I'm sure," she answered. "He told me in the confines of my room last night. And then only after I tricked him into it by demanding to know what he'd been doing lately. I threatened to tell Mama and Pa if he didn't. That's when he figured that he had no choice."

"Well, I guess I might have done the same in that predicament," Buck responded.

Lucy quickly mounted her horse and started to ride away. However, after prodding her mount for a few steps she pulled up abruptly.

"I want to thank you for what you've done for Cody. I'll always be grateful for it." With that said, she kicked the gelding and she was off.

As she rode back toward the ranch, Lucy pondered on what all had been said in that brief meeting. She knew Buck had done the right thing in telling her right off about his past. After all, he was just that kind of a man . . . thoughtful, polite, considerate . . . unlike most of the other cowboys. Still, the sting of it hurt her much, and she rode the last mile or two with tears streaming from her freckled cheeks.

Buck also thought about the meeting. He hated to hurt Lucy more than anything in the world. This family, the Thorns, was now more like his own family than any other he'd ever known. And what if he got over Kelly Stanfield? Had he ruined his chances of ever loving, and being loved, by another girl? Anyway, those were foolish thoughts because his heart still yearned to see her again. Still, his mind settled on the conclusion that he'd done right by Lucy in being honest with her. And he somehow sensed that she understood this. For this, he was thankful.

When Buck got back to the ranch that evening he decided to make no mention of Lucy's revelation of Cody spilling the beans. Rather, he decided to set the first stage of the trap by engaging Cody in an argument in front of the others. They had previously discussed this, and Cody knew to follow his lead. He chose the supper table to begin the scam.

"Cody, it looks to me like it's time you carried your weight around here," Buck began. "I'm tired of having to do work for the both of us."

All eyes around the table swung to where the two were seated.

"That's your opinion, MISTER Buck," Cody responded sarcastically. "I'll do as I dang well please, and you won't have any say in it."

"You're right there, boy," Buck retorted. "But don't count on me to cover for you anymore."

With that Buck slammed his fork down, grabbed up a couple of the made-from-scratch biscuits on the table, and headed for the bunkhouse. Buck was convinced that their little act had served its purpose. He'd noticed Jake watching intently as it unfolded, even noticing a slight grin on his face as Cody lit into him.

Buck spent the remainder of the evening lying on his bunk and visualizing the plan. He determined that tomorrow he'd tell Cody to apprise Jake of the Cains leaving town and that he knew where their stash was. He'd set the trap for the following night at the old Crenshaw place. If everything went right, they'd be rid of Jake for good.

Buck slept well that night, assured that his plan would work. He rose early as usual, ate, and quickly went to work out to the west from the ranch. At noon he noticed Mr. Thorn approaching on his mighty black stallion. You could always tell it was him from far away because he had to fight the big horse almost continuously to keep him out of a dead run.

"Mr. Thorn," Buck offered as he rode up. "Why don't you let me break that horse right for you. It'd be a heap more enjoyable to ride him if'n he was a little tamer."

"Much obliged, Buck," Mr. Thorn responded. "But I don't want to take his spirit away. Might as well ride a mare if I was going to do that."

Buck didn't argue any further, although he couldn't understand the reasoning. The two men simply discussed the plan again in its entirety, and Buck set the time for springing the plan. He asked Mr. Thorn to tell Cody to talk to Jake tonight, and to tell him the Cains would be back day after tomorrow. Tonight had to be the target.

"Are you sure you want to go through with this, Buck?" Mr. Thorn asked.

"I sure am. I wouldn't back down now for any amount of money." Buck answered.

"Well, we'll see you at the Crenshaw place shortly after dark, there on the road to town, where it makes the big turn to the north. I'll tell Cody to suggest that Jake sneak out of the bunkhouse sometime before midnight. That way no one could accidentally surprise us before we're ready."

Mr. Thorn made no more remarks. He simply mounted the stallion and muscled him in the general direction of the ranch, all the while trying to prove to Buck that he was no real problem.

The afternoon activities seemed to drag on and on. Buck was ready to face Jake, and the thought of just meeting him head on came to mind. But no, that wouldn't work. Oh, he could kill him all right, if Jake ever had nerve enough to draw. But they needed to prove to everyone what kind of character he was, and to run him out of the territory . . . or else kill him.

The thought of killing another man didn't appeal to Buck. He could remember all of those previous times, and never once did he feel good afterwards. But he knew this task needed to be done, and he was surely the only man to do it.

Buck didn't go to supper that night. Instead, he hung around the bunkhouse all evening. In his mind he wrestled with the plan and with his destiny in life.

Jesse didn't help much when he wandered in from supper. "A man that don't eat must have a girl on his mind. Kinda funny when you think about it, pardner."

"Jesse, you're a good friend, but you're way off on this one. Just leave well enough alone, would you?"

The tone of his voice caused Jesse to realize this wasn't the time for talking.

Buck grabbed the black Bible from under his bunk and began reading where he randomly opened it up. He had come to be amazed at how he could do this and almost certainly there would be some writing there that would speak directly to the circumstances he was currently in. This time was no exception. He read from the book of James where it said, "But the wisdom from above is first pure, then peaceable, gentle, reasonable, full of mercy and good fruits, unwavering without hypocrisy." This wisdom the Book talked about was what he needed now. Someone, or something, to tell him the right thing to do. And as he read further, he saw, "Therefore, to one who knows the right thing to do, and does not do it, to him it is sin."

This started his mind to questioning that which he was getting involved with. Should he back out? Would it be wrong in God's eyes if he were forced to kill Jake? Could he truly be a believer of God, and yet be willing to take another man's life?

His thoughts caused him to become startled when he realized it was dark outside. He knew he needed to get on the trail, and he needed to do it without much suspicion. So he quietly walked out the door, mounted Blaze who was still saddled and standing next to the corral, and headed to the Crenshaw place.

⌘

Chapter Fourteen

Buck rode slowly and deliberately through the crisp night air. His thoughts were on only one thing . . . the task at hand. Neither the starry sky nor the occasional cry of a coyote kept him from wondering what the upcoming confrontation would bring. He momentarily questioned the value of what he was doing; yet he ultimately concluded that it simply must be done.

He'd just passed Willow Springs, a rare oasis in this barren, parched land, when he saw a horseman up ahead, just visible under the full moon's light. With little difficulty he determined that it was Mr. Thorn, so he prodded Blaze on until he was within earshot.

"Hold up there, Mr. Thorn," Buck hollered.

"Man, you scared me half to death," Mr. Thorn answered. "Didn't know you were back there."

"Guess you had your mind too much on reining in that stud of yours," Buck joked.

"Don't get me started on that," he replied. "We got more important business to tend to right now." He said this with a hint of lightheartedness.

"I've a hunch this time tomorrow we'll be rid of Jake for good," Buck offered. "What do you think about that, sir?"

"I hope you're right, Buck," he said as the two drew even with each other. "I wasn't cut out to be a fightin' man. Oh, I've been in my share of scrapes all right. But not this kind of thing, where it could be a matter of life or death. And I guess I'm as worried for Cody, Lucy and Mama as anything. Don't want this thing to backfire and spill over on them."

"Don't worry, Mr. Thorn," Buck answered. "I hate to say it, but I'm used to these things, and I always seem to have a way of working them out in my favor. Expect this one will be no different."

"Buck," Mr. Thorn responded. "You never have really told me about your past. Is it really all that bad?"

"Well, sir, I wouldn't call it bad, but I once was told by a friend of mine, one of the few I really ever had, that I was always in the wrong place at the wrong time. That ain't too far from the truth. But the good Lord saw fit to give me some fightin' skills that others don't seem to have. Guess that's about all I can tell you now 'cause we got more important work to do, and pronto."

Two roads, rutted badly from years of wagon travel, joined together just ahead of the two men. Buck urged his mount to the left and toward the Crenshaw place as Mr. Thorn did the same. All the while Buck's mind was going over and over what the night might behold. He'd always had a peculiar way of visualizing what he was about to do. Like when he was a kid just learning to throw and spin a rope. He'd go over and over it in his mind until it seemed like he was actually doing it. On one occasion he entered a roping contest back home in Corsicana and he practiced and practiced until he just knew he'd win. He visualized the event in his mind . . . even about what the calf would look like. And sure enough, when it came his time he roped and tied the calf in record time, and the calf was marked just like he'd imagined him to be!

He was now visualizing the confrontation with Jake. His mind had already determined the outcome. It remained to be seen whether or not it would turn out to be accurate.

Buck was brought back from this daydream by Mr. Thorn's voice. "This looks like as good a place as any to hold up 'till they get here. What do you think, Buck?" Mr. Thorn asked. "I said, what do you think?"

"Uh . . . oh, sorry sir," came his surprised response. "Guess you caught me in one of my deep thinkin' spells. Was goin' over in my mind what the confrontation might be like. But I agree, this place looks fine to me."

The two men reined their horses over to a small clump of trees on a hill overlooking the Crenshaw's cabin. There they would be concealed from the band of thieves, yet they could spring from hiding at the right moment, and create the surprise that would be necessary.

"What kind of wait you expectin'?" Mr. Thorn asked.

"I figure it must be eight by now. They'll probably show up in two or three hours. I expect we'll git tired of each other's company by then," Buck added.

The men tied their horses to a couple of trees. Buck normally did not tie Blaze but he couldn't take a chance on him wandering into sight. Afterwards, they found a place to sit, talk and wait.

"Mr. Thorn," Buck started. You never know how these things are gonna turn out, so I'd like to tell you a thing or two."

"Sure, Buck, go ahead," he answered.

"First off, I'm right proud to have rode for you. Your family is the closest thing I've had to my own for some time now. I appreciate what all you've done for me."

Mr. Thorn interrupted. "Wait a minute, Buck. You're talkin' like you're leavin' these parts for good after this scrape."

"That's right, sir," he responded. Just let me finish my story and you'll know why. As I was sayin', I've grown close to your family and one thing has happened that I didn't count on. Lucy has kinda taken a likin' to me. To be honest, she's a great girl, one any rider would be proud to be hooked up with. But the fact is, part of that past I haven't told you about involves a girl. Aw, she dumped me good, but I still love her. Don't know if I'll ever get over her, and I told Lucy that myself. I'd be no good for her. Anyway, she deserves better than me. But when this is all over I'll be leavin'. Guess I'll make my way on to those New Mexico mountains I've always longed for."

"But Buck, that ain't no reason to leave. Lucy will get over you, and you never can tell but that you'd get over that girl, too, and you two might hit it off. I'd be right proud if she did rein you in."

"No, Mr. Thorn, that ain't possible. You see, a man told me one time that I'm just one step from glory, and he told me that 'cause I nearly got my fool head shot off. Fact is, trouble just follows me, and if I was with Lucy she'd be destined for heartache. So, I've reconciled my life to one of lonely driftin', just catchin' a glimpse or two here and there of happiness. I'm glad to say one of those glimpses has been here at the Lucky 4."

"Buck, I'm right proud to have had you ride for me," Mr. Thorn responded. "You're shore the best cowhand the Lucky 4 has ever had, and now you're savin' Cody from a life of tryin' to stay one step in front of the law. No matter what happens in this deal, Buck, I'll always be grateful for you steppin' in and doin' what you knowed was right."

There was little talkin' from that point on. The two men passed the time by looking at the stars, listening to the sounds of the night, and thinking of what was ahead of them. This caused time to pass by rather slowly, too slow for Buck.

"I think I hear them," Buck finally whispered to Mr. Thorn. "Let's get into position."

"You must be dreamin', Buck," he replied. I ain't heard nothin' yet."

About that time the sound of horses' hoofs and muffled voices came clearer. Buck had been right, and they were already closer than he thought.

Although it was dark, Buck took no chances that they'd be seen. He quickly moved toward the cabin, hunched down behind some old, empty whiskey barrels. Mr. Thorn followed closely, yet had much more difficulty moving quickly and quietly in that position. However, the two, in just a few moments, came to the place where they'd predetermined that Mr. Thorn would hide. It was a place of good cover, one where they were certain that he'd not be seen.

Buck moved on to the other side of the cabin. This proved to be a taller task than expected, for a couple of reasons. First, the night was so clear and the moon so bright, there were places where his silhouette could easily be seen. In these instances he hid at strategic places, and then bolted to cover as fast as possible. Once he thought he had been discovered, yet after a short wait he realized that it was only his imagination. Second, the animals were a problem. As in every plan like this one, there always seemed to be some detail that was overlooked. Such was the case here. The Crenshaws had taken their team of mules, and one broken-down mare with them. But the two or three chickens, an old lap dog, and a farm cat remained. It took considerable maneuvering to make it past them without alarming the fast approaching group of outlaws. Nevertheless, he managed to do it, and set up watch against one of the small out buildings located just a few yards from the cabin's front door.

Buck wasn't sure how many of the boys would be in on this heist. However, he could tell that his hopes were answered when he saw only three horses walking slowly in the direction of the cabin. Yes, he was right, one was Cody, one was a recently hired hand named Cole, and then there was Jake. They'd obviously left a lookout or two on the trail, but Buck wasn't worried about them. He figured they'd hightail it out of those parts if there were any gunfire to be heard. After all, riding in on a fight in the dark would be risky indeed, and this kind of men thought more of saving their own hides than they did in saving someone else's.

The three riders dismounted at the hitching post and calmly tied their horses there. Buck was shocked that they seemed to be almost careless in their actions. It was an indication that the setup had been successful. Cody had definitely convinced Jake that there was nothing to worry about. That's where he made his first mistake.

"OK, men," Jake announced in somewhat of a whispered voice. "Let's do it as planned. Cole, you stay here on the porch and keep a watch. Cody, you'll get your first taste of an actual robbery by comin' with me. Now, let's get on with it."

As soon as the two disappeared into the front door of the cabin, Buck moved quietly to a spot where he was only a few feet away from the lookout, Cole. He was doing a poor job of keeping watch. Rather, he was busy trying to find the makings for a smoke when Buck pushed the cold barrel of his Colt up against his right ear.

Although startled, the man didn't let out a sound.

"If'n you don't wanna see your maker real soon, you won't let out a peep," Buck whispered with a tone of coolness in his voice. "Now follow me, real quietly, right over here."

He quickly and quietly led the man, with the gun still at his ear, fifteen or twenty paces over to the barn. As soon as they rounded the corner and were out of sight of the cabin door, he hit Cole soundly with the Colt's handle. The ruffian dropped to the ground, unconscious.

Buck walked back out into the open and motioned toward Mr. Thorn to indicate that he was all right. He then took the place of Cole and positioned himself on the porch to await Jake and Cody's exit. It was then that the trap would be fully sprung.

Buck had time to do some thinking as he waited patiently on the porch. He knew his time at the Lucky 4 was drawing to a close, and he was going to miss it more than a little bit. Sure, he was basically a loner, primarily enjoying the solitude of being alone. But this Thorn family had grown on him. He was proud to be a part of helping Cody go straight. He appreciated the confidence that Mr. Thorn had showed in him on the ranch. And, he was more than honored to have drawn the attention of Lucy, although he had cut that relationship short.

He heard voices from inside the cabin and could tell that the two were about to emerge from the door. He stepped aside so that they wouldn't immediately see him, hiding on the east porch now rather than right there in front of the door. Since the porch to the cabin went all the way around it, he had no trouble positioning himself in this way.

"Well, Cody, my boy, you're now a real part of the gang," Jake announced as they stepped from the inside of the cabin.

"Thanks, Jake," Cody answered. "That makes me feel real special."

As soon as they stepped into the open Buck spoke up, with his gun pointed at the outlaw leader. "That may be true, Jake, but this gang's done for."

The surprise of Buck's voice caught Jake totally off guard. For what seemed to be a long moment, he just stood there, holding the bag of loot that had been placed in the house, and trying to figure out what to do next. The voice was unmistakably that of Buck Ward, and he knew, firsthand, what Buck could do with a gun. However, there were two of them, assuming that the lookout had been caught. Maybe he still had a chance, if he could get him out into the open.

"I might have known it'd be some Bible-totin', good boy who would try to stop me," Jake barked out.

Buck was surprised at the coolness that Jake displayed. Perhaps he'd mistook him for less of a man than he really was.

"You're right there," Buck answered. "But now ain't no time for talkin'. Drop your gun right now if you want to see the light of the mornin'. We got you surrounded and them guards up the trail ain't gonna be no good to you here in this fix."

"I ain't fallin' for that trick, Buck," he answered. Besides, me and Cody here can take you on by ourselves."

"Cody, are you willin' to risk your life to run with this trash?" Buck responded.

"I believe not," Cody said as he backed off from Jake. "Guess I'll sit the rest of this one out."

Jake's reaction to this newfound dilemma was to utter several obscenities, leaving the best of them for Cody and his backstabbing ways.

"Never you mind there, Mr. Jake," Buck interrupted. "Now, how about droppin' that firearm, and I mean pronto."

Buck wasn't prepared for Jake's next move. Primarily because of the darkness, but some because of his overconfidence in Jake's cowardly nature, Buck was caught by surprise.

As Jake drew his pistol from its holster he came up firing. The first shot hit right beside Buck, blasting a corner of the house away right beside his ear. At the same moment Jake took to the woods, with only a stray shot from Mr. Thorn falling harmlessly late. He disappeared into the night on the dead run.

Mr. Thorn arrived immediately, clutching Cody in his arms. "Thank God you're all right. How about you, Buck?"

"Ain't nothin' hurt here but my pride. I can't believe I let that snake get away."

"Well, he's gone," Mr. Thorn announced. "We did what we came to do. He won't show up around here anymore."

"That's where you're wrong, sir," Buck countered. "Jake's been double-crossed, and he ain't the type to let it go by. I've got to go after him."

With that Buck hit the woods on a dead run, gun in hand, prepared for the worse. He was no fool, and he knew that hurrying off into dark woods after a man who knew he was coming was not a wise thing. Still, something told him to go, and he had a calm assurance that if he did, he'd get his man.

The woods were too dark to pick up any kind of trail. His only hope was to find his way as quickly as possible and try to make up some ground on the robber. He estimated that Jake had about a minute head start. It had taken about that amount of time to gather his wits and speak briefly with the Thorns.

Once into the woods, the trail became fairly clear, especially so for the nighttime. The clear sky and the bright moon accounted for that, so Buck was able to move faster than he expected. He didn't think that Jake would venture far from the beaten path, unless he was going to lay in wait and spring a trap of his own. If that happened, Buck might be a goner.

He had run for about two minutes when he thought he noticed movement to his side. He instinctively dove into some cover to his left and landed with a jar. It was none too soon, for he felt the whiz of a bullet graze the side of his face as he came to a halt. Although momentarily startled, Buck knew that fate was now on his side. Jake could have hidden in those woods all night if he'd taken a mind to, yet now he'd revealed his whereabouts. Now, they were playing on Buck's terms.

Buck quickly rolled several times, all the while with his Colt in his hand, and came to rest up against the trunk of a tree. Another shot landed about three feet to his left, an indication that Jake now was uncertain exactly where he was. This revelation caused Buck to think momentarily about that fight with the two Indians, and how both parties were striving to know where the other one was.

He'd noticed the flare of Jake's gun in the darkness and surmised that Jake was still in his original position, just off the beaten trail. Buck guessed that he must have some good cover there or else he'd be moving himself. Twice more in the next thirty seconds a shot rang out, from the same location, with each one falling further away from Buck.

There was no doubt about it now, Jake was scared. He'd missed in his prime opportunity to catch Buck while unaware of his location. Now he was shooting just to calm his anxiety and to maybe get in a lucky shot.

Buck decided to stay put for a while. He figured that Jake would stay put, and if he could lie still enough for long enough, he might cause him to make a stupid move. He might even convince Jake that one of those blind shots had found its mark.

Lying still for an extended period of time was no problem for Buck. He'd learned to do so, in life or death situations during the war. More than once he'd eluded the enemy's pursuit by simply finding a suitable spot and making no move. He'd then move out in the opposite direction when danger passed.

But this time he planned to lie still until Jake made the move. He knew he could wait him out, so he just assumed a comfortable position, with his back up against a tree to hide his silhouette, and waited.

His thoughts raced during this period of waiting. He thought of his childhood, his hometown of Corsicana, of Lyle the blacksmith, the Thorns, and . . . yes, he thought of Kelly Stanfield, too. And it seemed like a long period of time passed before anything else happened, when actually it was only a few minutes.

At first the movement from the other side of the trail was slow and deliberate. Although Buck couldn't see all of what was happening, it was evident that Jake had lost track of where Buck had last been. He was actually moving in a direction toward Buck, instead of the other way! Either he thought he'd hit him, or he had become disoriented in the dark and didn't know exactly where he was.

Buck just waited. The shadowy form of Jake came closer and closer, all the while unknowingly falling into Buck's second trap of the night. And this trap had no way of escape.

Momentarily Buck could make out Jake's movements clearly. He had his gun in his hand, and he was backing down the path, thinking that danger lurked on the trail that he had already covered. That's when Buck spoke up.

"If you move another inch I'll bore you," Buck spoke in a semi-whisper voice.

The shock of Buck's voice startled Jake, yet he did not immediately make any sudden movement.

"Now I'm gonna tell you again, like I did before. Drop that pistol if you want to see the light of day."

During all of this Buck had still never changed his position. He sat with his back to the tree and gun pointed at Jake.

"Well, I guess we'll never know who's faster now," Jake countered, figuring to perhaps trick Buck into making a move he'd later regret.

"Won't work, Jake," Buck responded. "I don't need to prove myself with the likes of you."

At that moment Jake whirled in a flash. Just like at the cabin earlier in the night, he caught Buck off guard. But this time his move didn't end up the same. As Jake turned, Buck released the hammer on the Colt. It only took the one shot. Jake would raid no other homesteads in that part of the country. And he would ruin the lives of no other young men.

⌘

Chapter Fifteen

Once again Buck and Blaze moved toward New Mexico alone. The monotonous flat plains in the upper Texas panhandle yielded little scenery for him to gaze at, so his thoughts were of the past.

His departure from the Lucky 4 had been a sad one for him. He rode back to the ranch after the shooting only to get his belongings and to say a brief goodbye. There was a handshake with Mr. Thorn, a hug from his wife, a good-natured encounter with both Cody and his favorite cowhand, Jesse. And then there was Lucy.

Lucy ran toward Buck as he was mounting to ride away. It was true that he planned to leave without speaking to her. He thought it would be best that way.

"Leaving without saying anything to me?" she asked with a slight tone of anger in her voice.

"Guess you got me there," Buck answered. "Figured it might be better that way."

"And just why do you think it'd be better that way?" she again questioned.

"Well, you know, after our little talk, I just thought...."

Buck didn't get anything else out before Lucy interrupted him.

"That's one thing I hate about cowboys. They always think they know what a person is thinking and what they might want. Well, you'll never know what I want before I wish for it. Keep that in mind, Buck Ward, as you ride off on another one of your escapades to escape your love for that girl back home."

Those words angered Buck, but before he could respond he realized they were true.

"I guess you've got my whole life figured out," Buck responded.

"Enough so that I know you won't ever be happy 'till you get her out of your system."

With that Buck was taken aback by Lucy's abrupt kiss, right square on the lips.

"Now remember that when you get lonely out there on the prairie and there's no one around for you to be close to, except that horse you adore so much."

Lucy stomped off toward the house, without looking back.

Right before she reached the door Buck hollered, "Thanks." That was the last word he said to any of the Thorns, and he realized afterward that it summed up his thoughts about that family mighty good. They had been good to him and he was grateful for it. He particularly appreciated Lucy's clumsy efforts to show her appreciation and to make an effort to convince him that she, although still caring for him, could now move on to other things.

Buck's plan was to move on with much haste so that he could reach the mountains and get settled in before the cold winter hit. He was anxious now. It had been quite a spell since he first left Corsicana, and he didn't want to waste anymore time. He now had ample provisions, had a good stash in his money belt and had a horse that was ready to be on the move.

He reached the main road heading north shortly after noon. After only a brief stretch of lonely riding he looked off to the east and noticed a dark cloud maybe a mile or so off. It was the strangest looking storm cloud he had ever seen, looking more like dust that anything else. About that time he thought about the descriptions of the commotion a huge buffalo herd could arouse, and he decided that he had to go take a look. After all, he'd heard that the big shaggies were being killed off and he might never get another chance to see so many in one place.

Blaze, once more his sole companion, didn't act too thrilled to be heading in that direction. It was almost as if he could sense that this diversion might delay the two from reaching their destination. Nevertheless, he loped off in the direction Buck decided on and it wasn't long before he could hear the roar of the big, black monsters running for their lives.

Buck had heard about the speed of a bison. It was hard for him to imagine that an animal so big and bulky could travel at such a fast speed. He had been told that for a short while a buffalo could out-distance a good horse. This he determined to test for himself.

When they got within a half-mile of the stampede Buck could begin to make out what was happening. With nothing between him and the buffalo but the wide-open plains, he saw what proved to be a sickening sight. There were riders, bunches of them, chasing the mighty animals and shooting them with high-powered rifles. The black monsters had no chance, for the riders would merely ride up to their sides and make a straight shot right to their heads. The plains were strewn with black specks for as far as he could see, an indication that this slaughter had been going on for quite a while. As Buck got closer to the action, the dust became stifling to him, so much so that he had much difficulty breathing.

It was at this point that Buck didn't know what to do. His first thought was to pick off one or two of the riders and maybe make them give up for the day. He then envisioned an opportunity to ride through the heart of the herd and try to move some of them in a different direction. He gave up on both thoughts, deciding instead that it was simply too much of a job for one man. Still, the dust, the blood and the stench of the dying carcasses spread out for miles made him sick. He simply couldn't leave the scene without at least making his thoughts known.

At about that time, something caused the men to quit pursuing. It was almost as if someone had just waved a wand to bring it to a halt. But for whatever reason, they stopped and the herd kept on running to what they considered safety. He knew that that was not the case.

A group of the hunters, or more like slaughterers, gathered just a little ways from where Buck now stood watching. He decided to call on them, but knew to be careful. These hide hunters, as some folks called them, were known to be a filthy, lawless bunch. Yet Buck's conscience made him ride into the midst of them.

As he approached all eyes were on him. There looked to be about six or eight of them, and they struck him to be just as he'd heard. They wore buckskin, all of them, most had long, shaggy hair and beards, and he could smell them as he approached. Most didn't have handguns, at least that he could see; yet they all grasped at their buffalo guns as he rode up.

"Howdy," Buck yelled as he rode in, careful to stay far enough away that he could keep an eye on all of them at one time.

There was no response from any of them for quite some time. Finally, the one who looked to be the leader said, "What is it you want here, stranger?"

"Nothin' much," Buck answered. "Just never had a close look at this kind of operation before, and thought I'd get my fill."

"Well, there ain't much to see, and we'd feel a whole lot better if you got your education from somebody else," the leader said.

Buck's inclination was to try to set these men straight on what they were engaged in. The ridiculous slaughter of animals, simply for economic gain, certainly didn't set well with him. Yet, for one of the first times in his life, he felt the urge to move away from, instead of toward, trouble. He realized that he couldn't buck this size of a group, and there were men like these all over the plains.

"You're probably right," Buck responded. "I've seen all I need to see anyway."

With that Buck turned Blaze back toward the west, gave him a good kick in the flanks, and quickly made a getaway.

As he rode back toward the road north he contemplated the move he'd just made. Perhaps it was possible for him to avoid trouble. Maybe this was the Lord's way of telling him that. It was just possible that the killing of the outlaw Jake

Cord was the last act of that kind that Buck would ever know.   Maybe, just maybe, New Mexico and the glory of the mountains would be the right medicine for him.   The medicine to heal, the medicine to forgive, and the medicine to forget.

Before he knew it Blaze had carried him back to the main road, and he was traveling northwest toward his beloved mountains.   Many times during this trek, and even before that, Buck had imagined what the Rockies would look like.   Everyone he'd asked had told him that you couldn't describe them in words.   They told him they would first appear as clouds on the horizon, something he really couldn't understand.   After all, if you stop and think about it, how could mountains appear to be clouds?   They then told him that as you got closer and closer to them they'd appear to change in color, in dimension, and in beauty.   Finally, when you were really close, they'd appear to be impossible to cross.

He came back to the reality of the plains he was now crossing.   This desolate country was not appealing to him at all, except that the absence of trees enabled him to see far off on the horizon.   He'd taken after someone from his childhood that he once heard say, when in the deep woods of East Texas, "Ain't there anyplace around here where a man can see off?"   He loved to look as far as the eye could see and imagine what was out there ahead.   And he knew that before too many more days passed, that "what" out there would be the Rockies.

Buck talked to Blaze as they moved on like he did in days gone by.

"Blaze, ol' boy, won't be long now before this long trek will be over.   You're not gonna know how to act when you get in them mountains.   I'll bet you'll have to grow a heavier coat to keep them bones warm.   What d'ya think."

Of course, as always during these conversations, Blaze did not respond.   He only continued to carry his owner across the prairie as no other horse could do.

After three days of constant travel Buck decided to get off the main road for a spell. He'd not seen a human being since leaving the buffalo hunters, and he had no desire to do so. Yet, he needed some supplies, and a crude sign with an arrow pointing to the east told him it was only eight miles over to Dry Gulch, a name Buck thought to be fitting for the area. He reined Blaze in that direction, and with no hesitation at all, he took off as his master asked.

The country changed little in this direction. Little grass, cactus, the ever-present Texas tumbleweeds and small clumps of greasewood were about the only vegetation around. He remembered thinking that he was glad he'd toted extra water when it happened.

A loud rattling sound, one that could only come from a diamondback, startled Blaze as they bottomed a small, dry creek bed. Uncharacteristically, Blaze let out a loud response and reared up, causing Buck to crash down to the ground in a violent manner. He landed with a thud, first on his right leg, and then falling to the ground, headfirst.

At least four hours passed with Buck still unconscious. It was now close to dark, and he aroused to a body full of pain, literally from his head to his feet. He knew enough about doctoring to know that he'd suffered a concussion, and he quickly formed an opinion that his leg was broken just below the knee. Walking was impossible, so Buck decided to crawl to a suitable spot and stay for the night.

He glanced to his right and saw Blaze munching on some prairie grass. He whistled, and just as always, he came running. After much painful maneuvering he was able to unsaddle Blaze and get his bedroll and blanket. He then fell asleep.

"Hey, mister, somethin' the matter with you?"

At first Buck thought he was only dreaming, but he then realized that this was a real voice coming from a real man. The man was old, having obviously weathered many winters out in the elements. He had a long, gray beard that stretched almost to his waist. His voice was strong, yet age had had an effect on his vocal cords, and he sounded much like the grandpa he remembered from his childhood. The oldtimer had on a heavily soiled hat, a pair of blue colored britches, and suspenders holding them up. Behind him was a grey donkey, heavily loaded down with belongings, looking as though he would just as soon be there as anywhere else in the world.

The man again spoke before Buck came to his senses. "Mister, I said, is somethin' the matter with you?"

"Shore is," he began. "Horse got spooked by a rattler, pitched me off, and broke my leg. I was out for a few hours, and when I waked up all I could muster the strength to do is get my horse unsaddled and lay down. Guess I been asleep for a good while now."

"Eh," the old man muttered. "Expected as much. You young'uns don't know how to make it out here in the rough. You're lucky I came along. Probably won't be anybody else by here for a week or more. Road's only used by two or three folks, and then only when they're goin' in for supplies. A body could die right here on the road and nobody would ever know it."

"Well, I'm much obliged to you, Mister . . . Don't guess I caught your name. Mine's Buck."

"Folks around these parts call me lots o' names, most of 'em of an unkindly nature. You can call me by my Christian name, Lucas," he responded. "Now, what is it I can do to get you out of this scrape?"

"Don't suppose there's a doctor in that town up ahead?" Buck asked.

"Ain't one for a hundred miles," he answered. "But my woman's at the house, and some folks say she's better at fixin' folks' ailments than any of them city doctors out east. If you're up to it I can help you get there, and we'll put you up 'till you're healed enough to travel. Where you headed anyway?"

"The mountains. Hadn't planned on stoppin' for more'n one night 'till I got there," Buck responded.

The old man's eyes lit up when Buck mentioned the mountains. "What business you got traipsing' up to God's country?"

"No particular business," Buck said. "Just want to see 'em. Guess I ain't never been more'n a hundred feet high in my life."

"Well, boy, you're in for some good, and some bad times, if'n you're plannin' to stay there for a spell. Them mountains stretch as far north as a man can imagine. There's snow and avalanches. There's wild animals - bears, mountain lions and the like. There's places where the travel is impossible, where that there horse you're ridin' won't even attempt to cross. But on the other hand, there's the handsomest lakes and rivers you ever seen. There's wildlife for the takin'. The beaver are thick, the deer and elk just invite you to take 'em, and the trout . . . them trout are the best fish a man ever put in his mouth."

"Mr. Lucas," Buck began. "You sound like a man that knows what he's talkin' about. You used to live in them mountains, I suppose?"

"Most of my life," he answered. "Only in these last few years have I been stuck in this godforsaken land. Course, that's a story better saved for later. Right now, I expect you and me need to figure out how we're gonna get you to the place. It's a good two miles out across that ridge there," he said, pointing to the southwest with his finger.

"I think I can ride, that is, if we go awful slow," Buck said. "That poundin' that I normally enjoy will be the death of me if we don't take it easy."

"No problem, boy," the old man responded. "I ain't got nothin' but time, and travelin' afoot the way I do takes a heap of time. But, you know, I always figured that it helped me be ready for anything . . . anything physical that is."

With that the old-timer grabbed up Buck's rigging and walked over to Blaze, who was standing only a few yards away.

"Never had much use for horses," he said. "Scared of anything that moves, eat more'n a man can feed 'em, and can't go to lots of the places I want to go. But this shore is one of the handsomest I've ever laid my eyes on."

"Won't find one any better," Buck said frankly. "He's hauled me out of more'n one scrape."

It didn't take the old man long to saddle and bridle Blaze, so he turned his attention to Buck. "Now, how we gonna manage this?"

"Just give me a minute and I think I can get stood up. If I can manage that, you can lead ol' Blaze there over to me and we'll figure out the rest."

The man did as he was told. Blaze neighed gently when he brushed up against Buck, seemingly understanding that his companion of so many years was now in a fix. Buck, standing on his one good leg, took one leap up to land, belly first, across the saddle. He let out a loud yell indicating that the pain associated with this move was tremendous.

"I ain't much for cussin'," Buck uttered. "But that hurt enough to change my attitude on that!"

"Sometimes it's good for a man to let off some steam. What you got against swearin' ever now and then?" the stranger asked.

Before Buck answered he somehow managed to swing his good leg over the saddle and come to a somewhat natural riding position. He emitted another loud cry of pain and then answered the old man.

"Been readin' the Good Book a lot lately," he began. "There's a part in there that says a man shouldn't take the Lord's name in vain. A body told me one time that that meant cussin'. Got me to thinkin' about what a man gets out of swearin'. I couldn't come up with one good thing."

"You're a strange boy," the man stated. "Mama may be sore that I brought a preacher home with me. She don't take too kindly to religion."

"Don't worry," Buck responded. "I ain't a preacher, at least not now, anyway. I won't try to force any religion down your throats. You can count on that, especially if'n you take care of me the way you said you would."

With that, Lucas handed Buck the reins and motioned to start off in the direction of the place. In turn, he grabbed the burro's lead rope and started that way too, without even looking to see if Buck was managing all right.

The going was plenty rough for Buck. Nothing jars a man as much as riding a horse, and Blaze didn't know any easy way to take steps. Every move he made transferred itself right to Buck's hurt leg. Every now and then a particularly big jolt hit him and he let out with a scream of pain.

"Ahhhhh!" Buck yelled particularly louder than some of the other times.

"Hurt, does it, young feller?" the old man asked. "Well, this here predicament reminds me of the time I was up there in them mountains you're lookin' for. Got my leg broke just like yours, only a heap worse. Why, I couldn't have even crawled up on a horse if'n I had one, but I was afoot, as usual. Must'a been close to zero that day, snow drifts as high as your head, and the wind howlin' like a wolf cryin' for food."

"How'd you hurt it?" Buck asked.

"Got it caught in a bear trap," he replied. "Worse pain I ever had. Took me almost a day in that cold weather just to get it out. Then I had to more or less crawl to safety. Finally found a dry spot under some rocks, and low and behold there was some dry wood there that somebody else had stacked up. If'n I was gonna believe in that God of yours, that was one of those times. Guess we all look to somethin' else when we get ourselves in that kind of fix."

"You're right there, old-timer," Buck answered, but refusing to say anymore after remembering his pledge to not talk about religion too much.

As the old man continued walking to the southwest Buck couldn't help but begin wondering how he and his woman got out here. The man had told him that he didn't like this country, yet here he was, crossing the red sand and passing the occasional greasewood bush in a methodical manner.

"Why'd you leave the mountains?" Buck blurted out.

"Ain't no place for ol' folks," he began. "My bones got to hurtin', my joints started achin' and my wife started complainin'. Guess I always knowed that it'd come to a time when I had to live a gentler life. But I shore do miss them spectacular cliffs and the beauty of lookin' off into a valley and seein' for miles. If'n you ever get there, you ain't gonna regret the trip."

"Ain't no doubt I'll get there," Buck stated. "Guess now, though, it'll be a little longer than I planned on."

The two said little after that, and Buck contented himself with merely looking out across the vast prairie and taking in the effect of nature. It was almost noon now, and Buck reckoned that they should be getting close to the old man's house.

Just about then the trail took a sharp turn to the right, and when they rounded the turn Buck caught his first glimpse of the house, or more like a shack. It was standing up against a small mound, probably twenty or thirty feet high. Buck estimated that it couldn't have been more than about ten by fifteen feet in size, and it was just about the crudest shack he'd ever seen. The walls seemed to be leaning with the slope of the land, and the roof appeared that it couldn't have stopped much water. The window on the front was uncovered and the door was wide open. A crudely built fence stood on one side of the house, and it looked like a couple of hogs were rooting toward the back of the enclosure. One milk cow was roaming loose, right next to the pen.

The old man never said anything as they approached. It was as if there was no use to make any introduction or to call out to his wife that he was coming.

"That you, Lucas?" a voice from within called.

"Who'd you expect it was, the governor?" he answered in a sarcastic tone.

There was no immediate answer to this. However, by the time the two men reached the yard, a haggardly old woman appeared at the cabin's door.

"Have a good trip?" she asked the old man, totally ignoring the fact that Buck had ridden in with the man.

"Guess so, 'cept I ran across this young codger in a heap of trouble. Rattler spooked his horse and he took a fall. In purty bad shape when I found him. Reckon you could look him over?"

Buck wasn't so sure now that he wanted this woman doctoring on him. She was surely as old as the man himself. She wore a faded gray, gingham dress that was as dirty as it was gray. Her hair was a mess, and she was barefooted. You could tell that arthritis had taken its toll on her, for she walked stooped over and her hands were misshapen from the effects.

"Now that he's here, guess I got no choice," she answered.

Buck mustered all his strength and somehow managed to get off Blaze and stood on his one good leg.

"Ma'am, I appreciate your offerin' to help, but I really think that rest is most of what I need," Buck said.

"Naw," the woman said bluntly. "You need a splint on that leg, and I'm gonna have to set it first."

Buck couldn't remember ever having a broken bone before, but he'd heard stories about havin' to put bones back in place. He imagined the pain that he'd have to endure, and he knew that from looking at his injury it was a severe one. The thought of this old woman being in charge of his mending didn't set too well with him.

She helped Buck to the door of the shack and told him to go in and lay down flat on the bed.

Buck entered the cabin and immediately noticed a very unpleasant smell. It appeared that cleanliness was not high on this lady's list of priorities. The place was cluttered with everything they owned, and there were few shelves or hooks to hang anything on. The bed was over in the corner of the one room, right under one of the two windows.

Buck let out a loud yell as he allowed himself to fall to the bed. The pain was becoming familiar to him now, but it still hurt just as much. And, as he lay still just for a few moments, he found himself fighting an urge to go to sleep. This made him realize that the ordeal he'd gone through had sapped him of his usual strength. No matter how he fought it, he couldn't stay awake. Within only a few moments, the stillness and the comfort of being on that bed caused him to fall off asleep before the old man and woman ever followed him into their abode.

"I'm plumb tuckered out," Grandpa said as he looked at the old railroad watch he carried in his pocket.

"You ain't gonna leave us right there, with Buck asleep on that ol' bed, are you?" I asked, with a tone of disgust.

"I sure am, and if you argue too much you'll have to figure out the rest on your own."

That was all that needed to be said.

The next day found us all seeming to go our separate ways. Herman was busy working on some cabinets that he was buildin' for Mama's kitchen. I looked on for a few minutes and wondered how he could make all the cuts come out so perfect. He definitely had a knack for woodwork. Frank went out to the creek bottom to shoot his .22 rifle. No one was a better shot than him. Mama fired up the old cook stove and started a pie abakin', all the while showing Mary Sue how it was done. And Poppa stayed all day long in that blacksmith shop, makin' new shoes for all the horses and mules.

Now, me, I saddled up ol' Roxie and took off with the wind. I never tired of ridin', and I particularly liked ridin' fast. And the only bad part was that when she got to coverin' that ground fast she was hard to slow down. Why once I thought I never was goin' to get her stopped and she ran me through some purty rough brush down on Chambers Creek before I got her excitement under control.

As Roxie and me were ridin' along that day my thoughts went forward. I wondered what life would be like for me in ten, twenty or even thirty years. Would I always be a loner like I was now? Would some purty young lady ever take a likin' to me? Would I ever marry and have a family?   Would I ever get to ride those rails like I sometimes dreamed of? Would I ever be able to perform my rope tricks like Tom Mix did?

I spent most of the day ropin' and ridin' and didn't get back home until midday. Poppa was standin' in the door of his shop when I rode in, and I could tell he had something on his mind.

"Travis," Poppa said. I got some paintin' for you to do. Get in here right now."

Even at this age I had a knack for paintin'. It was one job I didn't dread doin'. I guess it was because I could use some of my artistic talents, something that the school marm had bragged on me about.

"All right, Poppa," I answered. "Let me get Roxie taken care of and I'll be right there."

I spent the rest of the day workin' on that old dresser and mirror Poppa had told me to paint. He didn't say so right then, but I later found out he was sprucin' it up for Mary Sue to use. She didn't get much fancy stuff in those days and he wanted her to have somethin' nice for a change. Even though Mary Sue and I didn't always see eye to eye, for some reason I worked extra hard on that dresser so she'd be proud of it.

Mama hollered that supper was ready at the usual time and we all gathered round the table. After grace was said, a lot of the talk centered around the dance that was gonna be held in town the next weekend. The older boys were thinkin' about gettin' a chance with the purty girls, Mary Sue was dreamin' about dressin' up, and I . . . yes, I was thinkin' about ol' Buck.

"Grandpa," I said, interrupting the talk of the dance. "Why can't we get back to the story?"

"Not tonight," he said. There'll be another time for that.

I didn't like the answer, and it proved to be more than a week later before I got Grandpa to continue the story.

Chapter Sixteen

Buck awakened to see both the old man and the old woman standing over him. It seemed only a moment ago that he had dropped to the bed, but it was now dark outside, so he knew that hours had passed.

"Hated to wake you up," the old woman said. "But that there leg needs settin' and it's already been too long. Chances are you'll always walk with a limp if we don't get to work on it right now."

"Well, I guess I'm game," Buck said in response. "Let's get it over with."

"All right," she said. "Lucas has cut a couple of limbs off the only tree in this part of the country to use for splints. What we got to do is get that leg back in the right position, apply the splints, and then wrap it as tight as we can. If all works right, you'll be healed in a couple of months."

"Will it take that long?" Buck asked.

"Shore will, and could be longer if it's as bad as it looks," she said.

All the while the old man said nothing. Buck thought that this relationship was strange in more ways than one. They didn't even seem to like each other. Yet, here they were, living in the same house, and depending on each other for survival.

"Now," she began. "This is gonna hurt worse'n anything you ever felt before. Here's a shot of whiskey to take to ease the pain some."

"No thanks, ma'am," Buck replied. "Just give me somethin' hard to bite down on good. I can take it."

"As you please," came the response. "Lucas, hand him that leather quirt there. It should serve the purpose."

Lucas did as he was told and it was only a few moments before they were ready to begin the operation.

"Now, Lucas, you try to hold him down while I do this," she ordered.

When Lucas got in position as instructed, the old woman explained to Buck what was about to happen.

"I'm gonna do this in two moves. First, I've got to pull your leg straight down. I hope on one jerk I can move it into the right position. If so, I can then go to the break point and make the other move to line up the two bones right."

The old lady paused a moment and voiced, "Are you ready?"

"Get after it," Buck said as he bit down hard on the quirt.

At that moment the woman grabbed his foot on the bad leg and gave one mighty jerk.

"Ahhhhhhhhhhhhhhhg!" Buck screamed.

After a brief moment, when he got his senses back, he shouted, "Maybe I should'a taken a slug of that redeye."

"It's still here," she said. "But the worse one's now over. Ready for step two?"

"Ready as I'll ever be," Buck responded, still with his voice showing the pain he was in.

She then took hold of his lower leg at the break and shoved with strength that he couldn't believe a woman could muster.

Another yell emerged, and then the next orders came.

"Now, don't move a muscle," she said. "We were lucky. It looks like it went right back in place. Lucas, bring them splints over here right now."

The old man complied with the directives and Buck could see her place one on one side of his leg and the other on the other side. She began with the wrapping at about his ankle and started circling his leg and the splints until she had reached up above his knee. She then tied it off, started at that same place, and reversed the direction, ending up at the ankle. Again, she tied it off, and then started over. This went on until at least six or seven layers of wrapping had been applied. She then called for two smaller splints to place on the front and back of his leg. She commenced to wrap these in a similar fashion until another four or five layers had been accomplished. At that she announced the job completed.

"Now I'm gonna get some strong soup in you, and then you can finish that nap," she said with a wink.

"Sounds good to me," Buck responded. "Fact is, the pain's not near as bad as it was. A full stomach might help me some, and I know I could use some more sleep."

"Well, I'll rustle it up," she responded while walking to the other side of the room where the wood stove was.

Buck's thoughts began moving quickly as he lay there with nothing else to do except wait on his meal. He first thought of his childhood, then about his trek to this place, and then, yes, his thoughts moved to Kelly Stanfield. No telling where she was right now, and he was certain that he'd never see her again. In fact, stuck way out here in West Texas as he was, he might not ever see anyone that he'd known before. This thought seemed to disturb him some.

The meal came sooner than he thought, and he finished it up in a hurry. Truth was, that was some of the most awful tasting soup he'd ever put in his mouth. And he was plumb scared to ask what kind of meat was in it, so he just gobbled it up, swallowed hard with each mouth full, and hoped the old woman didn't expect him to eat any more.

"You must have really liked that possum soup," she said. "Didn't know if you'd eat it or not."

"Aw, it was good," Buck lied back. "But I'm plumb full now and ready for that shuteye you said I needed."

"Well, go ahead and get that rest," she replied. "It's near dark now anyway and Lucas and me will be hittin' the sack purty soon."

Buck followed her orders, thankful for avoiding any more of the soup, but more thankful for running across the old man and woman in his time of need. The truth of the matter was that she was good at doctoring and she'd set his leg as good as any town doctor would have, maybe better.

When Buck awoke the next morning the sun was already high in the sky. It wasn't like him to sleep so long but his injuries surely changed his routine. He looked around and saw no one in the cabin and heard nothing outside to indicate that the two were in the vicinity. He decided to try to sit up and he managed to do so with a minimum amount of pain, much less than he'd had the day before when he had to mount up on ol' Blaze for the ride to the cabin.

He really didn't know whether he needed to stay off his leg, but he decided it'd probably be best to avoid as much pressure on it as possible. That proved to be harder than one might expect, especially since Buck wasn't used to sitting around and doing nothing. It wasn't long before he decided to venture to the door and try to catch a glimpse of what was going on.

"Aiheee!" he said as he managed to get to his feet. A sharp pain went through his leg as he got up and he didn't know if he was going to be able to stand it. Just about the time he was going to sit back down on the bed he noticed a freshly cut tree limb shaped crudely like a crutch. It had some cloth wrapped around the top to soften the feel under his arms. The two old folks had left it there for him, probably knowing that he'd want to move around some when he woke up.

Buck struggled to use the crutch, something he'd never done before in his life. He shortly began talking to himself about his predicament.

"Can't believe the fix I'm in," he began. "I'm stuck out here in this godforsaken country with a broke leg and I don't even know how to use a crutch."

About that time he realized that he was talking, but no one was listening. He'd never before carried on a conversation with himself, and he decided right then that he wasn't going to start now.

He managed to get to the door with some effort and leaned up against the casing, half out of breath. He looked in all directions and never caught any glimpse of the two old folks. There was no telling where they were. Maybe they went to town. Maybe they were tending to their animals. Or maybe they were in back of the place doing some other chores.

"Anybody around?" Buck hollered. There was no response so he hollered again, but got the same result.

He decided to hobble down the steps of the porch and try to get a look at the back of the house. Since there were no windows facing that direction in the old shack, this was his only option.

Going down the two steps made him realize just how clumsy he really was. He'd always fashioned himself to be pretty nimble, especially when he had a rope in his hand. He could spin it around him, jump in and out of it while using either a flat or a butterfly motion, and could rope cattle effortlessly while sitting atop old Blaze. Yet, here he was in this predicament and he couldn't even handle a crutch to perfection. He guessed he'd figure it out sooner or later, and he proposed that it'd better be sooner.

He managed to get to the back of the house in a few minutes and he readily saw the old woman off in the distance. He guessed it to be at least four hundred yards to where she was and he couldn't really tell what she was doing.

When he started to yell out to her he realized that he'd never been told her name. He thought that to be strange, especially since Lucas had talked about her so much. When he thought about it for a while he remembered that the old man addressed her only as woman.

"Hello," Buck hollered with his hands cupped around his mouth. When he saw the woman look up and back at him he yelled again. "Wanted you to know I'm up and around," he declared.

The woman dropped what looked to be a shovel of some kind and started walking back to the shack.

"Don't stop on my 'count," he yelled in response to her movement. However, it had no effect on her as she kept walking with slow, deliberate strides.

When she got within easy talking distance, she spoke up.

"You need to get back in the shelter. Won't be good for you to move around too much this early."

"Thought you might say somethin' like that," Buck responded. "But I ain't much of one to stay put for too long."

"Well, you better learn," she answered. "That is, if'n you want to walk straight again in this lifetime."

Those words stuck with Buck pretty heavy. He'd never thought much about dying, and he had been prepared to do it on more than one occasion. But the thought of being crippled for the rest of his life scared him more than a little.

"Yes, ma'am," he said momentarily, as he began to turn and move back in the direction he came from. "I'll try to be a good patient for you, but I ain't promisin' to sit flat on my back forever."

The old woman slowly followed Buck as he stumbled clumsily back to the front of the house, up the steps of the porch and through the still open doorway to the cabin. In all, this must have taken at least three or four minutes.

"Looks like you got a lot to learn about being crippled," she said as she entered the room and Buck fell exhaustedly to the bed.

"Guess you're right, ma'am," he replied while gasping for air. "By the way, I ain't never heard you say what your name is, nor what you and your husband's last name is."

"Come to think of it, you're right," she replied. "Fact is, Lucas hardly ever calls me anything 'cept Woman, and I don't see too many folks way out here to have to tell. Even sounds kinda strange to tell you that I'm Irene, and our last name is Capp."

"Well, Mrs. Capp, I want to tell you again how obliged I am for you folks to take me in like this. I reckon I'd be in a heap of trouble right now if'n your husband hadn't come along."

"Don't mention it," she said. "You seem like a nice young man and we could do with a little company around here now and then."

"I don't mean to be pryin'," Buck said. "But I can't imagine what you were doin' out there behind the house while ago."

"You wouldn't believe me if I told you," she answered. "But I'll try it on you for size. We're lookin' for gold."

"That is a might bit hard to believe," he replied. "But I suppose you'd have no reason to lie to me about it. Had any luck?"

"Lucas would probably shoot me if he knew I told you this, but the fact is that we've made a livin' at it, but just barely. Lucas was comin' back from town when he found you. He takes the dust in ever so often, and always takes just a little at a time so it won't look like we've struck it rich. We figure our lives wouldn't be worth a plug nickel if folks knew much more than that about it."

"You're probably right," Buck stated. "But I didn't know there was any gold within a hundred miles of this place. How'd you strike onto it?"

"Was really an accident," she answered. "Lucas was out huntin' one day after we first came to these parts. He found the source of the dry creek bed that runs out behind the place, and noticed a yellowish tint to the sand there. He'd seen gold before in them New Mexico mountains and knew right off what it was. We been workin' that bed ever since. Guess we . . .er, uh, I've already said too much."

Buck sensed that the old lady had an uneasy thought about finishing the story.

"Ma'am," Buck began, "Don't you ever worry about me tryin' to horn in on your claim. I'll swear to you right now, on a stack of Bibles, that your secret is safe with me. The good Lord has blessed me over the years with all I need in the way of money and belongins', and I shore ain't gonna try to take what ain't mine."

"Thanks, young man, but I'd still be obliged if you wouldn't tell Lucas right off that I blabbed all this."

"You can count on that, Mrs. Capp," Buck stated firmly. "I won't bring it up at all unless you give me the word."

The events of that day turned out to be repeated over the next several weeks as Buck slowly but surely began to improve. He spent much of his time reading his Bible as Mr. and Mrs. Capp methodically went about their work looking for gold. Buck never said a word to Mr. Capp that he knew and the old man never mentioned it for himself. Once during this period of time the old man packed a bag, loaded it on his mule and headed off in the direction of town. Still, Buck never questioned him about his activities and Mrs. Capp never mentioned the subject again.

One day Buck was particularly bored with his eventless existence, so he decided to write his friend Lyle a few lines.

Dear Lyle,

I take pen in hand to write you this letter. I'm still in Texas. Had a bad accident. Got threw from my horse and brok my leg. Was taken in by some nice folks livin here in the panhandle. They been nice to me but I'm almost heled now and ready to move on to them mountains. Lyle, ain't nothin gonna keep me from gettin there as soon as I'm well.

Hope things is goin well for you there in Ft. Worth. Has it grown any since I was there?

Lyle, you don't know how nice it is for a cowpoke like me to have a friend like you to write ever now and then. Wish I had a girl, but I guess I won't ever git over Kelly.

If'n I ever git somewhere for good, I'll send my address. Otherwise, I'll keep in touch.

Buck

When he finished the letter he addressed it and put it aside to give to Mr. Capp the next time he went to town. But the writing of the letter had gotten him into a somber mood, and he knew why. It was the mention and thought of Kelly Stanfield.

No matter how hard he tried, he could never fully get her out of his mind. Even when reading his Bible each day he would come across something that jarred his memory about her. Like the time he was reading about two sisters named Mary and Martha. Buck couldn't help but compare Kelly to Mary, the sister who paid the most attention to Jesus. Or, on another occasion, he was reading the Old Testament and he came upon a story about Sampson and Delilah. Buck thought Kelly to be a modern-day version of Delilah.

Time with the Capps passed quicker than Buck realized. One afternoon he announced to Mrs. Capp that he thought it was time to rid himself of the cast on his leg. He was totally surprised when she immediately agreed.

"Can't believe you ain't said somethin' before this," she said. "It's been more'n six weeks now."

Although the time had passed boringly slow for Buck, he didn't know it had been that long since the fall.

"You ain't lyin' to me, are you?" he asked.

"Son, you ought to know by now that I ain't the lyin' type," she said, although realizing all along that she was just joshin' him.

"You know what I'm gonna do first when I git this thing off?" he asked.

"Probably a lot of scratchin'," she replied.

"Well, that's right, but not what I had in mind. I'm gonna go saddle up ol' Blaze and hightail it outta here for a long ride. I know he's probably been as bored as I have all this time."

About that time Mr. Capp came in the door to the cabin.

"What's all that loud talkin' I been hearin'?" he asked.

"We're celebratin'," Buck quickly answered. "Gettin' my cast off today."

"About time," the old man stated as he walked back out the door.

"What's botherin' Mr. Capp?" Buck asked the old woman.

"Truth is, that old man of mine has takin' a likin' to you, son," she began. "You see, we ain't never had no kids of our own, and the fact of the matter is we ain't never had any close friends. Since you came here Lucas has enjoyed your company. Guess he was hopin' you might stay on a while after you healed."

"I never figured on stayin, ma'am," he replied. "Although I guess I do owe y'all somethin' for all you've done for me."

"You don't owe us nothin'," she stated abruptly. "You're a kind and good boy. That Bible readin' of yours has had a good effect on both of us. We got to thinkin' that we been by ourselves for so long that we didn't need nobody else. But your bein' here made us understand the errors of our ways. Fact is, I been readin' from our ol' Bible to Lucas late at night myself. Since he can't read hisself, I have to do it if'n he's gonna ever know its words."

"Ma'am, that's about the best thing anybody ever said about me," Buck stated with a big lump in his throat. "I won't ever forget that you're the first two folks I could say that I've had that kind of influence on. Makes me right proud."

"Aw, let's get away from this mushy talk," the old lady said. "Let's get that leg back to normal."

She went over to the cupboard and grabbed a pair of scissors to use to cut away the bandages.

"Git over there on that bed and straighten that leg out toward me," she ordered.

Buck did as instructed and she started cutting away the bandages. He didn't realize how dirty the outer ones were until he saw the clean ones that had been hidden underneath. Layer after layer came off until he saw his crinkled, ash white skin. He had a hard time believing that that was his leg. It didn't feel the same either. In fact, Buck had a sensation that somethin' far more serious was now wrong with his leg. But Mrs. Capp eased his mind by telling him that it was only natural for him to feel that way. That was a real relief for him.

When she was finished she told him to stand up and put some weight on it. He did this and had trouble balancing himself at first. But as he tried to take a few steps he got better at walking, and the stiffness and slight pain began to go away. Although not normal, it sure was better than lugging that cast around and having to use that homemade crutch.

"Mrs. Capp," Buck said. "You missed your callin'. You should have been a doctor."

"Aw, ain't nothin' lots of others couldn't have done," she responded. "Now get outta here and try out that leg. Won't hurt nothin' to walk on it for a while."

"What about ridin'?" he asked.

"Go ahead and try it," she said. "My belief is that the minute you take that cast off you're better off really exercisin' the leg."

With that Buck headed out of the old cabin. Although limping all the while, he went down the steps to the porch and straight to the corral where Blaze was standing.

"Ol' boy," he began. "Are you ready to get back to some normal livin'?"

Blaze let out a whinny as if he understood exactly, so Buck patted him on his big, strong neck and saddled and bridled him. With only a slight winch of pain, he mounted up and started off in the direction of the dry creek bed in search of Mr. Capp. However, before he got out of shouting distance, Mrs. Capp hollered out at him.

"Got my permission to talk to the ol' man about the gold. It's time he knew." With that, even before Buck could give a response, the old lady returned to the house.

The afternoon air was hot and dry as it usually was during that time of the year. That didn't bother Buck, though, for the thrill of once again riding in the open air was all that he could think about. He'd missed it much, and he realized at that moment how anxious he was to get back on the trail to New Mexico. He decided right then and there to leave early the next morning. But first, he wanted to set things right with the old man.

Buck led Blaze toward the foothills while still following the creek bed. It was only a couple of minutes before he spotted Mr. Capp, bent down on his knees, digging in the dry dirt of the bed.

"Say, Mr. Capp," Buck hollered. "Mind some company for a while?"

"Expect not," came the reply.

With that Buck drew to a stop and dismounted. He walked the brief way over to where the prospector sat, now on his backside.

"Mrs. Capp told me about your gold find," he started. "Sounds like you been mighty lucky."

"Luck don't have nothin' to do with it," he remarked back. "Been doin' this kind of thing for nigh on fifty years now. I got a knack for findin' it."

"Well, I just want you to know that your secret's safe with me. I'll be leavin' at first light in the mornin' and you won't have to worry about me anymore."

The old man looked at Buck with teary eyes.

"You ain't been no trouble to us," he began. "As a matter of fact, I grown to like havin' you around. The ol' woman and me been purty lonely over the years. We both, without really sayin' it, hoped you'd stay on. But I understand how a boy your age needs to be on the move. Was like that once myself."

"Mr. Capp, you folks have treated me just like one of your own. I just want you to know how much I've appreciated your takin' me in and carin' for me. Don't know what I would've done if'n you hadn't happened along when you did. Fact is, I might even be dead right now."

"Aw," the old man responded. "Don't make more of it than there was. You'd have done the same for me if the situation called for it."

Buck could tell the old timer was struggling to keep back the tears. He then did something he'd not done in years. In fact, he didn't remember ever doing it. He hugged the old man with all his might.

"Mr. Capp, you been like a father to me over the last few weeks. I just want you to know how much you mean to me."

Buck said these words and released his grip on him at the same time. The emotion hit him all at once. Tears welled up in his eyes and both of the grown men just stood there, right out in the middle of nowhere, sobbing and talking about their relationship.

"Son," Mr. Capp said. "I ain't never felt this way before about a boy like you. If I had a son, I'd want him to be just like you."

"Mr. Capp," Buck responded. "Fact is, if you knew all about my life you might not feel that way. I've done more'n a few things that I'm ashamed of. In some ways, I've been cursed, and in other ways I've been blessed."

Buck went on to tell the old man most of his life story. He didn't leave much out, detailing his troubles brought on by gunplay, telling about his sad home life while he was growing up and ending with his story about his love for Kelly. In all he must have talked for more than an hour, probably the longest he'd ever spoken in his whole life.

It was late afternoon when the two completed their talk. The sun had moved from overhead to the west, and the heat was bearing down on the two of them as they sat in the red, West Texas sand.

"Son, don't feel bad about them times. Sounds like you always used your gun for good, if you can put it that way. I know you've had a good effect on the old woman and me. Now, I want to show you something. Let's take a little walk."

Buck didn't say anything as he began following Mr. Capp up over a small rise on the horizon. They were walking due east, and must have traveled about a half mile when they approached an outcrop of rocks jutting up from the sand. It looked almost like the rocks had been placed there by someone, but he knew better. It was the handiwork of God himself. The old man walked around the base of the rocks and stopped when it appeared that the red and yellow colors converged. At this spot there were several flat sandstones, some almost two feet across, lying on top of each other.

"Son, I ain't never showed anybody this before, not even the old lady.

Buck's mind began wondering what he was about to see. Maybe it was going to be something left by the Indians of long ago, perhaps some pottery or an arrow or club head. Maybe it was where an animal lived and the old man wanted him only to see it. Or, just maybe, there was something valuable there. Buck couldn't reach any conclusion about what he predicted it would be until Mr. Capp had moved four or five of the heavy stones from on top of each other.

"There it is, boy, take a look."

Buck peered into the opening with great anticipation. His eyes widened quickly when they adjusted to the dark environment and he realized what he was looking at. It was gold! More than he'd ever seen or heard of in one spot before. There were nuggets, some the size of a good-sized tomato, like he used to pick in Corsicana. Others were smaller, but just as valuable. Then there were several bags tied up with horsehide strips. They evidently contained either dust or very small nuggets. All in all, Buck figured there must have been enough gold stashed there to buy up the whole state of New Mexico.

"Wow," he exclaimed. "I ain't never dreamed of seeing that kind of money in my lifetime. How'd you ever come by all of it?"

"Found ever ounce of it myself, that is, with the help of the ol' lady," he answered. "But she don't know how much we got of it. Was afraid if'n she knew she might want to leave these parts and make me move to town somewhere. That'd probably kill me right there. But lately, I been realizin' that it weren't fair to her to keep it from her. I'm gonna show her tonight, and I wanted you to know, too. Fact is, I want to give you a stake of it to help you make sure you reach them mountains."

"Mr. Capp, I couldn't take. . ."

"Don't tell me you can't take any of it," the old man interrupted. "A good boy like you needs a break here'n there, and this is yours. And I got another word of advice waitin' for you."

"What's that, sir?"

"I want you to go back to where you come from before you hit the trail up to them mountains. Why, you're just a young'un, and you got plenty of time to find that girl and then the both of you can head up there. Boy, from what you been tellin' me, you'll be miserable all your life if you go on without her."

Those words hit Buck strong. He knew that Mr. Capp was speaking to him straight. And he also knew that the old man was right, yet his pride forced him to argue.

"Mr. Capp, you don't understand the situation," Buck responded. "That girl ain't no count, and I 'spect I ain't no better. I killed more men already than I should, and that girl left me for a no-account drifter. No tellin' where she is now anyway."

Buck said these words, but deep in his heart he felt the need to do just what the old timer was suggesting. He longed to see Kelly again, and he'd give just about anything to hold her again, to see her beautiful black hair, and to hear that voice that had haunted him now for so long.

"Boy," Mr. Capp argued. "You're harder headed that any mule I ever owned. I'm tellin' you right now, you're doomed to be a lonely wanderer all your life if'n you don't listen to me and your heart right now. Take this money and high tail it outta here."

With that the man reached into the hole and flipped him two of the bags of gold, one at a time. He caught them, one in each hand, and was shocked by their weight. He knew right then that the old man was right, and that he really should go back for Kelly. But, his pride told him otherwise.

⌘

Chapter Seventeen

True to his word, Buck left at first light the next morning. Few words were spoken as he departed, but none of the three were unaware of the relationship that had been formed. He had tried to express it to them, but emotion got the best of him, so he simply mounted up and rode south.

Buck had no real intention of riding back to Corsicana to find Kelly. Yet, he didn't have the heart to say that to Mr. Capp, so he rode in that direction anyway. He was just about out of shouting distance when he heard a holler from the old man.

"Tell Kelly to treat you right," he yelled at the top of his lungs.

Buck waved a hand in the air to let him know he'd heard. He didn't look back.

The morning air was cool and crisp and Blaze was hard to hold back. It'd been a while since they had been out for any length of time and Buck could tell the mighty horse sensed a long trek was in store.

"Slow it down a little," Buck spoke to him. "We ain't in no hurry, 'specially since we're fixin' to turn and go the other way."

They must have traveled a mile or two from the Capp place when Buck began veering back around toward the north. He figured to hit the main trail headin' to New Mexico before long, and he hoped he wouldn't see another human being for quite a spell. He needed time to think, and he did his best thinkin' while sittin' atop a horse.

His thoughts were many, yet they always came back to Kelly. He knew Mr. Capp was right. But what if he went all the way back there and she was gone. Might've left with another two-bit tenderfoot. It'd take weeks to get there even if he rode hard. Then, what about his dream of the mountains? He might not ever make it, and, next to his love for the black-haired girl, this was his most passionate desire.

He spotted the road just ahead, but something caught his eye off to his right. Out of the sand, he saw a big boulder jutting out. As he got closer his curiosity got the best of him. There was something different about this rock. It looked like a tree, yet he knew that wasn't what it was.

"By golly, Blaze," he exclaimed. "That there is a tree that's turned into a rock."

He'd seen petrified wood before down around Corsicana. But those were usually just small pieces, some even hard to identify as having been wood. This one was fully seven or eight feet long, at least the part you could see was. It must have been two or three feet in diameter. The thought that this rock was a tree many years ago thrilled Buck and it set him to thinking about the glories of God's universe.

He dismounted and began walking around the boulder and touched it in two or three places.

"Blaze," he muttered, "I wish I could tote this rock to them mountains with us. If I could, I'd look at it everyday and realize how powerful God is, and that he can do anything he wants. Fact of the matter is, he's made me realize that my life ain't never gonna amount to much if I keep usin' my gun for the wrong reasons."

Something came over Buck at that moment. He fell to his knees and found himself cryin' out to the Lord for mercy. He'd never felt the presence of the Lord so close before, and it was almost as if he heard a voice saying, "Follow your heart, not your mind."

The experience left him shaking. He didn't understand how it had all happened so fast, yet he was unmistaken in what it all meant. He had to head back and try to find Kelly. And at the same time, he had to find a way to give up his gun.

With tears still in his eyes Buck mounted back up on ol' Blaze, took one last look at the magnificent boulder protruding from the west Texas sand, and headed south once again. This time it was not to deceive anyone. This time it was for the right purpose. This time it was for Kelly, and for a new way of life.

Buck and Blaze hit the road within about five minutes and were on their way back when he spotted a wagon headed for them. It was still a long way off in the distance, but it was clear to Buck that it was probably a family headed for what they hoped was a better life. A rider was atop a black horse slightly in front of the wagon, and two cows were trailing it, more than likely tied to it with a rope.

He started to veer off the road and to avoid having to visit with the strangers. He was now in a hurry to get home; that's all he wanted to do. But leaving the road would take more time, and he figured that the meeting would only last a few minutes.

The rider approached at a gallop and offered a friendly greeting when he got within speaking distance.

"Howdy, stranger," the man yelled. "Where you headin'?"

"Goin' south," Buck answered. "All the way to Corsicana. How 'bout you and your family?"

"New Mexico country," came the response. "Me, my wife and two daughters, and a girl we picked up on the way."

By then the two had reached each other and they both reined to a stop. The man on the horse was a friendly-looking man, with a straw hat on his head. He was slightly overweight, and had a face that reminded Buck of Lyle back in Ft. Worth.

"Where'd you start out at?" Buck asked.

"Comanche County," came the answer. "Indian trouble got the best of us. Heard it's a lot better out west."

"Guess it depends on what you're after," Buck said, as if he was an expert on the subject. "But I reckon there ain't no place right for you if'n your heart tells you you ought'a be someplace else."

"Them's mighty deep words comin' from a cowboy like you," the man responded.

With that, he reached across from the saddle and held out his hand for a shake.

"Name's Dan, Dan Holt. What's your handle?"

"Folks call me Buck," he answered.

The wagon was only fifty yards or so away now and the team of mules pulling it was working slowly and methodically on their way toward them. Buck noticed a small woman at the reins, and two little girls on each side of her. They looked to be about six or eight years of age.

"Hope you folks have a nice trip," Buck offered. "Weather's been good off in the direction you're headed. Nice to meet you."

With that, Buck poked Blaze in the ribs and started back on his journey. When he met up with the wagon he tipped his hat to the lady and spoke politely, "Howdy, ma'am." She only nodded her head and kept her eyes on the road ahead.

Buck rode on past the wagon, and had just about got out of shouting distance when he heard a call from that direction.

"Jeremy," a voice hollered. "Jeremy . . . Jeremy Ward."

Buck pulled Blaze to a halt as his heart began to pound rapidly. There was only one person that called him Jeremy, and that voice was unmistakable. It was . . .

"Jeremy, it's me. It's Kelly Stanfield," the voice returned.

Those words caused him to momentarily lose his thoughts. He sat atop Blaze in a blank stare. But then, just as quickly as he had lost his thoughts, the next thing he knew he was on the ground and running toward the girl, the girl who was running barefoot to him.

"Jeremy, oh Jeremy," she was hollering. "I've been looking for you for months. I love you."

Those words caused him to break his silence. His response came without thought.

"I love you, too."

In a moment the two came together and into each other's outstretched arms. Buck raised Kelly off the ground as he hugged and kissed her lips one, two, three and four or more times without thinking. He remembered the feel of her hair, the smell of the scent she wore and the softness of her skin. It all came back in a moment, as if they'd never been apart.

"Oh, Kelly," Buck uttered. "I've been so stubborn that I resisted my heart and left without you. I've always loved you, and just this morning I started back to find you. Never in my wildest dreams did I think I'd find you out here. Why, how'd you expect to find a drifter like me?"

"I don't know," she responded. "I just knew I couldn't live with the thought that I let you go without trying to find you. So I set out a couple of months ago to do that. When I got to Ft. Worth, I found out you had befriended Lyle the blacksmith, and followed your letters to the Lucky 4. They sent me in this direction, and I just hoped I'd find you. I met up with these nice folks a few days back and told them I was looking for a man in New Mexico. They let me ride in the back of the wagon. There's not much else left to tell."

"Oh," Buck spoke up. "There's a lot more to tell than that. But we've got a lifetime left for you to tell me, that is, if you'll accept my hand in marriage."

"Buck, those are the most beautiful words you could ever say to me," she said. "Let's do it in the next town, on our way to those mountains of New Mexico you're so interested in seeing. But first, I've got something I want you to see back at the wagon."

The two of them walked arm in arm back to the awaiting wagon. The whole family was standing beside it taking in the thrill of this chance meeting. They didn't say a word, just stood there with grins on their faces, realizing that it must have been the Lord himself that put those two lovers together.

They reached the wagon and Kelly rustled through her belongings until she pulled out a big gunnysack. She took it and handed it to Buck with a big smile of anticipation on her face.

"Go ahead," she ordered. "Open it up, it's for you."

Buck fumbled with the string that tied the sack, but finally managed to get it open. As he looked in he smiled and his eyes opened wide, the same as when he'd first seen Mr. Capp's gold. Reaching in, he grabbed hold of the finest pair of boots he'd ever seen, the same ones he'd wanted to buy out of that Ft. Worth store window. He sat down right there in the Texas sand and took his old ones off and struggled to pull the shiny new ones on.

"But, . . . how did you . . .? Buck stammered as he gazed at the boots in disbelief.

"Right before I left Ft. Worth I went back to tell Lyle that I was going to head west looking for you. He said he had somethin' for me to deliver to you if I didn't mind. And, well, there you have it!"

Standing up, Buck grabbed his bride-to-be and hugged her while lifting her off the ground. As he looked to the sky, he remembered his encounter with God just minutes ago. He then shouted, "Lord, I'm no longer one step from Glory!"

"Come on, Grandpa," I said. "Don't give us anymore of that mushy stuff. Tell us about what he did when he got to them New Mexico mountains. Did he really git rid of his guns? Did he like it when he got there? Did he ever git back to Corsicana? Come on, don't leave us hangin' like this"

"That story is for another time and place," Grandpa answered. "Right now you got chores to do, and the rest of us do, too."

"Aw, shucks. Just when we got to the good part."

⌘ The End ⌘

About the Author

Dr. Brian Nichols has been Dean of the School of Education since 2002 and is Professor of Education at East Texas Baptist University. His service to public school education began in 1973 as a teacher in DeSoto I.S.D. and progressed to positions as assistant principal, principal, director of business services in the Weatherford I.S.D., and superintendentcies in Elysian Fields I.S.D. and Marshall I.S.D. He has also held adjunct faculty positions at Dallas Baptist College, Stephen F. Austin State University and Texas A&M University at Texarkana.

Dr. Nichols is a native of Dallas, Texas and the fourth of five children. He is married to the former Paula Marie Matkin of Pittsburg, Texas and has two grown daughters, Kara Ann and Melanie Lynn.

Education is the only field Dr. Nichols has ever pursued. He is active in many professional organizations and has had articles published in statewide and national publications. He is an accomplished speaker and has presented numerous educational training sessions. His goal is to be a leader in the educational reform movement so that students can be better equipped to lead a quality life.

Dr. Nichols is an ordained deacon in the Southern Baptist church. He counts his role as the spiritual leader of his family as his most important responsibility.